The

Pirate Gow

An account of the conduct and
proceedings of the late John Gow alias
Smith, Captain of the late pirates,
executed for murther & piracy committed
on board the George gally, afterwards
call'd the Revenge; with a relation of
all the horrid murthers they committed
in cold blood; as also of their being
taken at the Islands of Orkney, and
sent up prisoners to London

by Daniel Defoe

with an introduction
by Nigel Rigby

NATIONAL
MARITIME
MUSEUM

Original spelling, grammar and punctuation retained throughout

First published in 1725

This edition published by
The National Maritime Museum, Greenwich, London SE10 9NF
www.nmm.ac.uk/publishing

Introduction © 2009, National Maritime Museum, Greenwich, London

ISBN 978-1-906367-23-7

A CIP catalogue record for this book is available from the British
Library.

Printed and bound in England by Cromwell Press Group

Mixed Sources
Product group from well-managed
forests and other controlled sources
www.fsc.org Cert no. TT-COC-2082
© 1996 Forest Stewardship Council
FSC

CONTENTS

INTRODUCTION

by Nigel Rigby

In 1814, the novelist Sir Walter Scott was travelling in the Orkneys where he later recalled meeting 'an old hag' who told him a tale about 'Gow the pirate, who . . . came to his native country about 1725 with a *snow* [a two-masted ship] which he commanded; carried off two women from one of the islands, and committed other enormities' before being captured by the islanders and sent to London, where he was tried and hanged. Recognizing a good story when he heard one, and adding material from Captain Charles Johnson's *A General History of the Pirates* (1724–28), which included a chapter on Gow, Scott incorporated both the pirate and the 'hag' into his novel, *The Pirate* (1822).

Some find even the best of Scott a little hard-going today, and it has to be said that *The Pirate* is not a sprightly read. It is chiefly remarkable for the way in which Scott takes the real, deeply unpleasant John Gow and turns him into the colourful hero, Captain Cleveland, the sole survivor of a pirate ship wrecked on Sumburgh Head. The charming but sinister Cleveland poses a threat to the islands, as did Gow, but by the end of the novel he redeems himself, repents his former life, joins the Navy and dies honourably. While Scott uses elements of Gow's story, Captain Cleveland is as much a part of a long romantic tradition stretching back hundreds of years. It is most famously exemplified by Johnson's *History*, a book which went through many editions and of which the modern historian of the subject, David Cordingly, has said 'publicized a generation of villains' from what has become known as the Golden Age of Piracy, giving 'an almost mythical status to men like Blackbeard and Captain Kidd'. The romance of piracy subsequently produced a long list of fictional heroes and attractive anti-heroes, from Byron's *The Corsair*, Gilbert and Sullivan's *Pirates of Penzance* (where the pirates are all noblemen who have gone wrong), R.L. Stevenson's Long John Silver, Burt Lancaster's athletic captain in *The Crimson Pirate*, to Johnny Depp's memorable Captain Jack Sparrow.

As *An Account of the Conduct and Proceedings of the Late John Gow* (1725) shows only too well, there was precious little romance in the true story of its subject, whose career as a pirate was nasty and brutish but mercifully short. It began in November 1724 with the bloody murders of his captain, first mate, the supercargo and surgeon on the *George Galley* off Santa Cruz (Agadir), and ended with his capture in the Orkneys and execution in London less than nine months later, on 11 June 1725. Gow had the misfortune to turn pirate towards the end of the 'Golden Age'. Piracy probably reached its height in the second half of the seventeenth century, briefly declined from the beginning of the War of the Spanish Succession in 1701, when the English government encouraged buccaneers to fight for their country, but flourished again with the ending of the war in 1713, when naval ships were laid up and seamen laid off. The government's attitude to freebooters had long been slightly ambiguous, with much shading around the edges of privateering (which was legal), piracy (which was not) and buccaneering (which wavered uncertainly between the two), but such was piracy's dramatic growth after 1713 that with the appointment of the ex-privateer Woodes Rogers as governor of the Bahamas, Britain declared a zero tolerance approach to it. Within ten years the most notorious pirates had been killed or captured and executed.

All executions were then popular public events and those of Gow and his crew were no exception. They took place at Execution Dock, Wapping, the traditional site where pirates were hanged at the low-water mark and their bodies left dangling for the washing of three tides. The *Dublin Journal* reported on 17 June 1725 that for Gow's execution the Thames was so crowded with small boats and that the 'prodigious concourse of persons' caused such 'mischief' that 'several lives [were] lost in the water and on the shore'.

According to the *Journal*, the pirates contemplated their imminent demise with insouciance, behaving 'themselves since their condemnation with an air of sensibility, and . . . under no apprehension of death or sense of their crimes'. The rope around Gow's neck broke after he had been hanging for four minutes and the anonymous author of the *Account* describes him mounting the steps to be hanged once more 'with very little concern'. This is very much how pirates were supposed to behave on the gallows, as careless of their own lives as they were of their victims'. However, another contemporary account has it that Gow 'beg'd heartily (tho' boldly), that he might not be hang'd again till the executioner whip'd him off and dispatched him with some thumps on the breast.' After being cut down from the gallows, pirates' bodies were customarily tarred and gibbeted (hung in chains to disintegrate slowly as a public warning to seamen) and this was the fate of Gow and his lieutenant, Williams, who were gibbeted facing each other on either side of the Thames near Greenwich.

Gow was twenty-eight at the time of his death. He was born in Thurso around 1697 and moved as a child to the Orkneys with his merchant father William and his wife Margaret, who brought him up in Stromness. Gow (Gobha in Gaelic) was once a common name in Scotland, the equivalent of 'Smith' in English. Many Gows anglicized their names to Smith from the early eighteenth century and this was the name that Gow assumed when he returned to Orkney in the captured *George Galley* in 1725. Legend has it that he ran away to sea, although exactly when is unknown, as is anything of his career prior to a first unsuccessful attempt to turn pirate on a ship homeward bound from Lisbon earlier in 1724, and his second successful attempt on the *George Galley* later that year. The *George*, a merchant ship of 200 tons and 26 guns, commanded by the Guernseyman, Captain Ferneau, was actually called the *Caroline* and identified as such by a merchant in the Orkneys, who had seen the ship a year earlier in Amsterdam. After the mutiny in which he seized her, Gow and his crew rechristened the ship *Revenge* and only changed the name to *George* on arrival in Orkney in order to avoid suspicion.

The *Account* of Gow presents a matter-of-fact picture of pirates, one which helps dispel many of the myths that have grown up around them. As his dispute with Williams shows, pirate captains were only as good as their last capture and had little job security; they were elected by their crews and could be replaced by a vote. Equally, a strong pirate captain was not afraid to act quickly and brutally to keep his position. Pirates were not merely lawless thugs, however, and their ships often had written constitutions. These were rather more than the 'guidelines' of the Pirates' Code in *Pirates of the Caribbean*, spelling out clearly the rules of behaviour and the punishments and rewards, in particular the 'share' of the plunder each man was to receive. Not all captured crews were slaughtered indiscriminately: Gow actually behaved rather well to his captives, allowing all of them to live. Crews were not always willing pirates: a large proportion of Gow's were effectively pressed men and their uncertain loyalty influenced a number of his actions. The escape of ten of the crew in the longboat in Orkney was the deciding factor in Gow's eventual capture. The plundering of canvas, rope and anchors from prizes, even when otherwise worthless, also points to the isolation of pirates living outside society and their need to be self-sufficient. Pirates could also be men of limited intelligence whose actions were determined more by chance and fate than cunning. Some of Gow's decisions were odd, to say the least, and while his determination to quit the Spanish and Portuguese coasts and refit in Orkney shows the rapidly diminishing number of pirate-friendly ports where ships could resupply and repair in the early eighteenth century, it was this misjudgement when compounded by basic navigational errors that led directly to his capture.

The episode there takes up more than half of the book. In many ways this is understandable as it was the public shock of pirates operating so brazenly and brutally in British waters that made Gow's capture such a *cause célèbre*. It is also in Orkney that the story moves from being told from the pirates' viewpoint towards that of the Orcadians, particularly Gow's captor and erstwhile schoolfriend, James Fea. The story did not end happily for Fea, however. He was lauded for his bravery and cunning in capturing a vastly superior number of heavily armed and desperate men, and was said to have received as a result substantial sums of money from the government, from the salvage of Gow's ship and from grateful merchants, but he was bedevilled and impoverished by law suits that followed in the wake of the case. In *The Real Captain Cleveland* (1912), his descendant, Allan Fea, tells how James espoused the cause of Bonnie Prince Charlie in 1745; in the reprisals following the Battle of Culloden his main house was plundered and burnt to the ground by Hanoverian forces, ironically meeting the fate that his house on Eday had escaped when he outwitted Gow.

The anonymously written *An Account of the Conduct and Proceedings of the Late John Gow* was published on 1 July 1725 by John Applebee of London. It was reprinted under the title of *An Account of the Conduct and Proceedings of the Pirate Gow* in 1898, in a limited edition of 250 copies. The editor, John R. Russell, then made two claims in his Preface: that the 'the only original copy that can be found is in the British Museum' and that the evidence that it was written by Daniel Defoe is 'unquestionable'. Russell was writing in good faith and using the best information available at the time, but he was wrong on both counts. A copy was also in Boston Public Library, USA, another is currently in Orkney Museum, Stromness, a fourth in the collections of Orkney Library and Archive and a fifth was discovered by the collector, Phillip Gosse, bound up in a fourth edition of *A General History of the Pyrates*. This, and the rest of his important collection of pirate literature, came to the National Maritime Museum's Caird Library in 1939 when it was purchased from him by the Museum's founding benefactor, Sir James Caird.

The belief that Defoe was the author goes back to the early nineteenth century. It was partly based on internal evidence of similarities of style with other works by Defoe, but also on the fact that Defoe worked from 1720 for the original publisher, John Applebee, who specialized in rogues' histories. The attribution was reinforced through the research of J.R. Moore in the 1930s, who attributed over 500 titles to Defoe.

The argument additionally depended on the fact that a short version of Gow's story had also appeared as a chapter in the third edition of *A General History of the Pyrates*, published a month after the *Account*, in August 1725. The *General History* is undoubtedly a key source for what we know today about pirates in the seventeenth and eighteenth centuries, but it too was first published anonymously, before the name of Captain Charles Johnson as author was added; and of Johnson nothing is known but the name. For J.R. Moore, the authors of both the *General History* and the *Account* are one and the same man, which is a reasonable assumption. Moore claimed, however, that 'Johnson' was in reality the pen-name of Daniel Defoe, who thus wrote both works.

This argument was questioned in the 1980s and 90s by P.N. Furbank and W. Owens, who reduced Moore's list of 500 works 'known' to be by Defoe by nearly half, to 290, and even questioned the fundamental assumption that Defoe worked for Applebee. Modern scholarship tends to follow Furbank and Owens' caution. In the most recent biography of Defoe both the *General History* and the *Account* of John Gow are excluded as being either 'not Defoe's or probably not Defoe's'. Nonetheless, the latest edition of the *General History* (reprinted in 1999) still attributes it to Defoe, although accepting that there is no proof of either position, and that this is now unlikely to be found. In my view, the arguments on both sides are strong, but perhaps it is best to forget them and enjoy instead the opportunity to read a great story that has been difficult to find for far too long.

Further Reading

Paula Backsheider, *Daniel Defoe: his life* (1989)

David Cordingly, *Life among the pirates: the romance and the reality* (2007 edition)

Peter Earle, *The Pirate Wars* (2004)

Allan Fea, *The Real Captain Cleveland* (1912)

Marcus Rediker, *Villains of All Nations* (2004)

Manuel Schonhorn, ed., *A General History of the Pyrates* (1999 edition).

Sir Walter Scott, *The Pirate* (1822)

THE PIRATE GOW

THO' this Work seems principally to enter into the History of one Man, namely, the late Captain John Gow alias Smith, the Leader or Commander in the Desperate and bloody Actions for which he has been Condemned; yet the Share which several others had in the whole Scene, and who acted in Concert with him, comes so necessarilly to be Describ'd and takes up so much Room in the Relation, that it may indeed be call'd the History of all the late Pirates so far as they acted together in these wicked Adventures.

Nor does the calling him (I mean this Gow or Smith) their Captain, denominate him any thing deeper in the

Crime than the rest; for 'tis eminently known, that among such Fellows as these, when once they have abondon'd themselves to such a dreadful hight of Wickedness, there is so little Government or Subordination among them, that they are, on Occasion, all Captains, all Leaders. And tho' they generally put in this or that Man to act as Commander for this or that Voyage, or Enterprise, they frequently remove them again upon the smallest Occasion, nay, even without any Occasion at all, but as Humours and Passions govern at those Times: And this is done so often, that I once knew a Buccaneering Pirate Vessel, whose Crew were upwards of 70 Men, who, in one Voyage, had so often changed, set up, and pull'd down their Captains and other Officers, that above Seven and Forty of the Ship's Company had, at several Times, been in Office of one kind or other; and among the rest, they had, in particular had, 13 Captains. Now, however, it was not so here; yet it seems, even in this Ship, Gow himself, tho' call'd Captain, had not an absolute Command; and was, at one time, so Insulted by Lieut. Williams, because he declin'd Attacking a French Ship from Martinico, that it wanted but little of Deposing him at that Time, and murthering him too.

In this Account, therefore, we shall have some Relation of the Conduct of the whole Ship's Crew, as well as of Captain Gow, nor will it, (I hope) make the work the less

Agreeable to the Reader, but the more so, by how much the greater Variety of Incidents will come in my way to speak of.

As to Gow himself, he was, indeed, a superlative, a Capital Rogue; and had been so even before he came to Embark in this particular Ship. And he is more than ordinarily remarkable, for having form'd the like Design of going a Pirating when he serv'd as Boatswain on board an English Merchant Ship, Bound Home from Lisbon to London, in which he form'd a Party to have seiz'd on the Captain and Officers, and to run away with the Ship: When, no doubt, had he accomplish'd his Work, the said Captain and Officers had run the same Fate as those did we are now to mention.

This I am so ascertain'd of the Truth of, that the Captain himself is ready to Attest it, to whom it was afterwards discover'd; that he, Gow, had made four of the Seamen acquainted with his bloody Design, and had gain'd them over to it: But not being able to draw in any more, and not being strong enough with these who he had so Debauch'd, they did not make their Attempt.

This, it seems, was not discover'd to the Captain, till after the Ship was discharg'd in the Port of London, and the Men paid off and dismiss'd; when Information being given, the said Captain endeavour'd to have apprehended

Gow and his Accomplices; but having (as t'was supposed) gotten some Notice of the Design, made off and shifted for themselves as well as they could, in which it was his Lot to go over to Holland.

Here it was, viz., at Amsterdam, that Gow ship'd himself afore the mast (as the Seamen call it) – that is to say, as a Common Sailor, on Board an English Ship of 200 Tons Burden, call'd the George Galley; he ship'd himself at first, as I have said, afore the Mast; but afterwards, which added to the great Misfortune, appearing to be an active, skilful Sailor, he obtain'd the Favour of being made Second Mate. The ship was commanded by one Oliver Ferneau, a Frenchman, but a Subject of Great Britain, being of the Island of Guernsey, to which also did the Ship belong, but was then in the Service of the Merchants of Amsterdam.

Captain Ferneau being a Man of Reputation among the Merchants at Amsterdam, got a Voyage for his Ship from thence to Santa Cruz, on the Coast of Barbary, to Load Bees Wax, and to carry it to Genoa, which was his delivering Port; and as the Dutch, having War with the Turks of Algiers, were willing to employ him as an English Ship, so he was as willing to be Mann'd with English Seamen; and accordingly, among the rest, he unhappily took on Board this Gow with his wretched Gang, such as

Maccauly, Melvin, Williams, and others; but not being able to Man themselves wholly with English or Scots, they were oblig'd to take some Swedes, and other Seamen to make up his Compliment, which was 23 in all; among the latter Sort, one was named Winter, and another Petersen, both of them Swedes by Nation, but as wicked too as Gow and his other Fellows were. They Sail'd from the Texel in the Month of August, 1724, and arriv'd at Santa Cruz on the 2nd of September following, where having a Super Cargo on Board who took Charge of the Loading and four Chests of Money to Purchase it, they soon got the Bees Wax on Board, and on the 3rd of November they appointed to set Sail to pursue the Voyage.

Thus much seems however proper to signify to the World, before they enter into the rest of Gow's Story, because 'tis evident from hence, that the late barbarous and inhuman Action was not the Effect of a sudden Fury rais'd in the Minds of the whole Company, by the ill Usage they had receiv'd from Captain Ferneau, in the Matter of their Provisions, or from their having over heard the said Ferneau threaten them when he spoke to the Mate, upon the Quarter Deck, to get small Arms into the great Cabbin, which they might suppose was in order to seize on them, and bring them to Correction, and so, in their Heat of Blood, might run them up to such a hight of

Rage as to commit the Murthers which they did not intend before.

But 'tis evident that this Gow, in particular, whatever the rest might have done, had entertain'd this bloody Resolution in General (I mean of turning Pirate) long before this Voyage; he had endeavour'd to put it in Practice, at least once before, namely, in the Ship (mentioned above) Bound from Lisbon for London, and had only fail'd for want of being able to bring over a sufficient Gang of Rogues to his Party; whether he had not had the same Design in his Head long before, that we do not know; but it seems he had not been able to bring it to pass till now, when finding some little Discontent among the Men, on account of their Provisions, he was made the Devil's Instrument to run up those Discontents to such a dreadful hight of Fury and Rage, as we shall find they did.

And this justly intitles Gow to the Charge of being the Principal, as well Author as Agent in the Tragedy that follow'd: Nor does it at all take off the Charge, that Winter and Peterson began the mutinous Language towards the Captain.

The Design must certainly have been laid among them before; how else should so many of them so easily form such a wicked Scheme in the few Minutes they had to talk together? Gow therefore is, I say, justly charg'd as Author of all the wicked Conclusions among them, and as having form'd a Resolution, in his own Mind, to turn Pirate the first Time he had an Opportunity, whatever Ship, or whatever Voyage he went upon.

AN ACCOUNT, &c

THE following Account being chiefly confin'd to the Conduct of this outrageous Pirate, Captain Gow, after his having actually turn'd Pirate, in this particular Ship, the George Galley, we must content ourselves with beginning where he began – that is to say, when they seiz'd the Captain, murdered him and his Men, and run away with the Ship, on the Coast of Barbary, in the Mediterranean Sea.

It was the 3rd of November, Anno 1724, when, as has been observ'd, the Ship having lain two Months in the Road at Santa Cruz, taking in her Lading, the Captain made Preparations to put to Sea, and the usual Signals for

Sailing having been given, some of the Merchants from on Shore, who had been concern'd in furnishing the Cargoe, came on Board in the Forenoon, to take their Leave of the Captain, and wish him a good Voyage, as is usual on such Occasions.

Whether it was concerted by the whole Gang beforehand we know not, but while the Captain was treating and entertaining the Merchants under the Awning upon the Quarter-Deck, as is the Custom in those hot Countries, three of the Seamen, viz., Winter and Peterson, two Swedes, and Maccauly, a Scotchman, came rudely upon the Quarter-Deck, and as if they took that Opportunity because the Merchants were present, believing the Captain would not use any Violence with them, in the presence of the Merchants, they made a long Complaint of their ill Usage, and particularly of their Provisions and Allowance (as they said), being not sufficient, nor such as was ordinarily made in other Merchant Ships; seeming to load the Captain, Monsieur Ferneau, with being the Occasion of it, and that he did it for his private Gain; which, however, had not been true if the fact had been true, the Overplus of Provisions (if the Stores had been more than sufficient) belonging to the Owners, not to the Captain, at the end of the Voyage; there being also a Steward on Board to take the Account.

In their making this Complaint, they seem'd to direct their Speech to the Merchants, as well as to the Captain, as if they had been concern'd in the Ship (which they were not); or, as if desiring them to intercede for them with the Captain, that they might have Redress, and might have a better Allowance.

The Captain was highly provok'd at this Rudeness, as, indeed, he had reason; it being a double Affront to him, as it was done in the view of the Merchants who were come on Board to him, and to do him an Honour at Parting; however, he restrain'd his Passion, and gave them not the least angry Word, only, that if they were aggriev'd, they had no more to do, but to have let him know it, that if they were ill used, it was not by his Order, that he would enquire into it, and that if any thing was amiss it should be rectify'd, with which the Seamen withdrew, seeming well satisfied with his Answer.

About five the same Evening they unmoor'd the Ship, and hove short upon their best bower Anchor, expecting the Land Breeze, as is usual on that Coast, to carry them out to sea; but instead of that, it fell stark Calm, and the Captain fearing the Ship should fall foul of her own Anchor, ordered the Mizen-top Sail to be furl'd.

Peterson, one of the malecontent Seamen, being the nearest Man at hand, seem'd to go about it, but mov'd so carelesely and heavily that it appear'd plainly he did not care whether it was done or no; and particularly, as if he had a mind the Captain should see it, and take Notice of it; and the Captain did so, for perceiving how awkardly he went about it, he spoke a little tartly to him, and ask'd him what was the reason he did not stir a little and furl the Sail.

Peterson, as if he had waited for the Question, answered in a surly Tone, and with a kind of Disdain, So as we Eat so shall we work. This he spoke aloud, so as that he might be sure the Captain should hear him, and the rest of the Men also; and 'twas evident, that as he spoke in the plural Number We, so he spoke their Minds as well as his Own, and Words which they had all agreed to before.

The Captain, however, tho' he heard plain enough what he said, took not the least Notice of it, or gave him the least room to believe he had heard him, being not willing to begin a Quarrel with the Men, and knowing that if he took any Notice at all of it, he must resent it and punish it, too.

Soon after this the Calm went off, and the Land-Breeze sprung up, as is usual on that Coast, and they immediately weigh'd and stood off to Sea; but the Captain having had those two Russles with his Men, just at their putting to Sea, was very uneasy in his Mind, as, indeed, he had reason to be; and the same Evening, soon after they were under Sail, the Mate being walking on the Quarter-Deck, he went, and taking two or three turns with him, told him how he had been us'd by the Men, particularly how they affronted him before the Merchants, and what an Answer Peterson had given him on the Quarter-Deck, when he ordered him to furl the Mizen-top Sail.

The Mate was surpriz'd at the Thing as well as the Captain, and after some other Discourse about it, in which 'twas their Unhappiness not to be so private as they ought to have been in a Case of such Importance, the Captain told him he thought it was absolutely necessary to have a Quantity of small Arms brought immediately into the great Cabbin, not only to defend themselves if there should be occasion, but also that he might be in a Posture to correct those Fellows for their Insolence, especially if he should meet with any more of it. The Mate agreed that it was necessary to be done, and had they said no more, and said this more privately, all had been well, and the wicked Design had been much more difficult, if not the execution of it effectually prevented.

But two mistakes in this part was the ruin of them all – 1. That the Captain spoke it without due caution, so that Winter and Peterson, the two principal Malecontents, and who were expressly mentioned by the Captain to be corrected, overheard it, and knew by that Means what they had to expect, if they did not immediately bestir themselves to prevent it. 2. The other Mistake was, that when the Captain and Mate agreed that it was necessary to have the Arms got ready and brought into the great Cabbin, the Captain unhappily bad him go immediately to Gow, the second Mate and Gunner, and give him Orders to get the Arms cleared and loaded for him, and so to bring them up to the great Cabbin, which was, in short, to tell the Conspirators that the Captain was preparing to be too strong for them if they did not fall to work with him immediately.

Winter and Peterson went immediately Forward, where they knew the rest of the Mutineers were, and to whom they communicated what they had heard; telling them that it was time to provide for their own Safety, for otherwise their Destruction was resolv'd on, and the Captain would soon be in such a Posture that there would be no meddling with him.

While they were thus consulting at first, as they said, only for their own Safety, Gow and Williams came in to them, with some others, to the Number of eight; and no sooner were they join'd by these two, but they fell down-right to the Point, which Gow had so long form'd in his Mind, viz., to seize upon the Captain and Mate, and all those that they could not bring to joyn with them; in short, to throw them into the Sea, and to go upon the Account.

All those who are acquainted with the Sea Language know the Meaning of that Expression, and that it is, in few Words, to run away with the Ship and turn Pirates.

Villanous Designs are soonest concluded. As they had but little Time to consult upon what Measures they should take, so a very little Consultation serv'd for what was before them, and they came to this short but hellish Resolution, viz., that they would immediately, that very night, murther the Captain, and such others as they nam'd, and afterwards proceed with the Ship as they should see Cause. And here it is to be observ'd that tho' Winter and Peterson were in the first Proposal, namely, to prevent their being brought to Correction by the Captain, yet Gow and Williams were the principal Advisers in the bloody Part, which, however, the rest soon came into; for, as I said before, as they had but little Time to resolve it, so they had but very little Debate about it. But what was first propos'd was forthwith engag'd in and consented to.

Besides, it must not be omitted, that as I have said, upon good Grounds, that Gow had always had the wicked Game of Pirating in his Head, and that he had attempted it, or rather try'd to attempt it, before, but was not able to bring it to pass. So he had, and Williams also had several times, even in this very Voyage, dropt some Hints of this vile Design, as they thought there was Room for it; and touched two or three Times at what a noble Opportunity they had of Enriching themselves, and making their Fortunes, as they wickedly call'd it. This was when they had the four Chests of Money on Board; and Williams made it a kind of a jest in his Discourse, how easily they might carry it off, Ship and all. But as they did not find themselves Seconded, or that any of the Men shewed themselves in Favour of such a Thing, but rather spoke of it with Abhorrence, they pass'd it over as a kind of Discourse that had nothing at all in it, except that one of the Men, viz., the Surgeon, took them up in short once, for so much as mentioning such a Thing; told them the Thought was Criminal, and it ought not to be spoken of among them. Which Reproof, 'twas supposed, cost him his Life afterwards.

As Gow and his Comrade had thus started the Thing at a Distance before, tho' it was then without Success, yet they had the less to do now, when other Discontents had raised a secret Fire in the Breasts of the Men; for now, being as it were Mad and Desperate, with Apprehensions of their being to be severely Punish'd by the Captain they wanted no Persuasions to come into the most wicked Undertaking that the Devil, or any of his Agents, cou'd propose to them. Nor do we find, that upon any of their Examinations, they pretended to have made any Scruples of, or Objections against the Cruelty of the bloody Attempt that was to be made, but came into it at once, and resolved to put it in Execution immediately – that is to say, the very same Evening.

It was the Captain's constant Custom to call all the Ship's Company every Night, at Eight a-Clock, into the great Cabbin to Prayers; and then the Watch being set, one Watch went upon Deck, and the other turn'd in (as the Seamen call it) – that is, went to their Hammocks to Sleep. And here they concerted their devilish Plot. It was the Turn of five of the Conspirators to go to Sleep, and of these, Gow and Williams were two; the three who were to be upon the Deck were Winter, Rolson, and Melvin, a Scotchman.

The Persons they had immediately Design'd for Destruction were four – viz., the Captain, the Mate, the Super Cargo, and the Surgeon, whereof all but the Captain were gone to Sleep, the Captain himself being upon the Quarter-deck.

Between Nine and Ten at Night, all being quiet and secure, and the poor Gentlemen that were to be Murther'd, fast asleep, the Villains that were below gave the Watch-Word, which was, who Fires next? at which they all got out of their Hammocks with as little Noise as they could, and going, in the Dark, to the Hammocks of the Chief Mate,

Super Cargo, and Surgeon, they cut all their Throats; the Surgeon's Throat was cut so effectually that he could struggle very little with them, but leaping out of his Hammock, ran up to get upon the Deck, holding his Hand upon his Throat, but stumbled at the Tiller, and falling down, had no Breath, and consequently no Strength, to raise himself, but dyed where he lay.

The Mate, whose Throat was cut, but not his Windpipe, had strugled so Vigorously with the Villain that attempted him that he got from him and got into the Hold; and the Super Cargo, in the same Condition, got forward between Decks, under some Deals, and both of them begg'd, with the most moving Cries and Intreaties, for their Lives; and when nothing could prevail, they beg'd, with the same Earnestness, but for a few Moments to pray to God, and Recommend their Souls to his Mercy; but alike, in vain, for the wretched Murtherers, heated with Blood, were pass'd all Pitty; and not being able to come at them with their Knives, with which they had begun the Execution, they shot them with their Pistols, Firing several times upon each of them, till they found they were quite dead.

As all this, before the Firings, could not be done without some Noise, the Captain, who was walking alone upon the Quarter-Deck, call'd out and ask'd what was the matter? The Boatswain, who, sat on the After Bits, and was not of the Party, answer'd, He could not tell, but was afraid there was some Body Over-board, upon which the Captain step'd towards the ship's side to look over, when Winter, Rowlinson, and Melvin, coming that Moment behind him, attempted to throw him Over-board into the Sea; but he being a nimble, strong Man, got hold of the shrouds, and strugled so hard with them that they could not break his Hold; but turning his Head to look behind him to see who he had to deal with, one of them cut his Throat with a broad Dutch Knife, but neither was that wound mortal. And the Captain still strugled with them, tho' seeing he should undoubtedly be murther'd, he constantly cry'd out to God for Mercy, for he found there was no Mercy to be expected from them. During this Struggle, another of the Murtherers stab'd him with a Knife in the Back, and that with such Force that the Villain could not draw the Knife out again to repeat his Blow, which he would otherwise have done.

At this Moment Gow came up from the Butchery he had been at between Decks, and seeing the Captain still alive, he went close up to him, and shot him (as he confess'd) with a Brace of Bullets.

What Part he shot him into could not be known, tho' they said he shot him into the Head; however, he had yet

Life enough, tho' they threw him Over-board, to take hold of a Rope, and would still have saved himself, but they cut that Rope, and he fell into the Sea, and was seen no more. Thus they finished the Tragedy, having murther'd four of the principal Men of Command in the Ship, so that there was now no Body to Oppose them; for Gow being Second Mate and Gunner, the Command fell to him, of course, and the rest of the Men having no Arms ready, nor knowing how to get at any, were in the utmost Consternation, expecting they would go on with the Work, and cut all their Throats.

In this Fright, every one shifted for himself. As for those who were upon Deck, some got into the Ship's Head, resolving to throw themselves into the Sea, rather than to be mangled with Knives, and murther'd in Cold Blood, as the Captain and Mate, &c., had been. Those who were below, not knowing what to do, or whose Turn it should be next, lay still in their Hammocks, expecting Death every Moment, and not daring to stir, least the Villains should think they did it in order to make Resistance, which, however, they were no way capable of doing, having no Concert one with another, nor knowing any Thing in Particular of one another, as who was Alive or who was Dead; whereas had the Captain, who was himself a bold and stout Man, been in his Great Cabbin with three or four Men with him, and his Fire-Arms, as he intended to have had, those eight Fellows had never been Able to have done their Work, but every Man was taken Unprovided, and in the utmost Surprise, so that the Murtherers met with no Resistance. And as for those that were left, they were less Able to make Resistance than the other; so that, as I have said, they were in the utmost Terror and Amazement, expecting every Minute to be Murthered as the rest had been.

But the Villains had done. The Persons who had any Command were Dispatch'd, so they Cool'd a little as to Blood. The first Thing they did afterward was to call up all the Eight upon the Quarter-Deck, where they Congratulated one another, and shook Hands together, engaging to proceed, by unanimous Consent, in their resolved Design – that is to say, of turning Pirates, in Order to which they, with a Nem. Con., chose Gow to Command the Ship, promising all Subjection and Obedience to his Orders (so that now we must call him Captain Gow), and he, by the same Consent of the rest, named Williams to be his Lieutenant. Other Officers they appointed afterwards.

The first Order they Issued was to let all the rest of the Men know, That if they continued Quiet, and offer'd not to Meddle with any of their affairs, they should receive no Hurt. But strictly forbid any Man among them to set a Foot

Abaft the Main-mast, except they were call'd to the Helm, upon Pain of being immediately Cut in Pieces, keeping, for that Purpose, one Man at the Steerage-door, and one upon the Quarter-deck, with drawn Cutlashes in their Hands; but there was no need for it, for the Men were so terrified with the bloody Doings they had seen that they never offer'd to come in sight till they were call'd.

Their next Work was to throw the three dead Bodies of the Mate, the Surgeon, and the Super Cargo over Board, which, they said, lay in their Way, and that was soon done, their Pockets first Search'd and rifled. From thence they went to work with the Great Cabbin, and with all the Lockers, Chests, Boxes, and Trunks. These they Broke open and Rifled – that is, such of them as belong'd to the mur-thered Persons; and whatever they found there, they shar'd among themselves. When they had done this, they call'd for Liquor, and sat down to Drinking till Morning, leaving the Men (as above) to keep Guard, and particularly to Guard the Arms, but Relieved them from Time to Time, as they saw Occasion. By this Time they had drawn in four more of the Men to approve of what they had done, and promise to Joyn with them, so that now they were twelve in Number, and being but 24 at first, whereof four were Murthered, they had but eight Men to be Apprehensive, and those they could easily look after; so for the next Day they sent for them all to appear before their new Captain; where they were told by Gow what his Resolution was, viz., to go a Cruising, or to go upon the Account (as above), that if they were willing to joyn with them, and go into their Measures, they should be well used, and there should be no Distinction among them, but they should all fare alike; that they had been forced by the barbarous Usage of Ferneau to do what they had done, but that now there was no looking back; and therefore, as they had not been concern'd in what was past, they had nothing to do but to act in Concert, do their Duty as Sailors, and obey Orders for the good of the Ship, and no Harm should he do to any of them. As they all look'd like condemn'd Prisoners brought up to the Bar to receive Sentence of Death, so they all answer'd by a profound Silence; not one Word being said by any of them, which Gow took, as they meant it, viz., for a Consent, because they durst not refuse; so they were then permitted to go up and down every where as they used to do. Tho' such of them as sometimes afterwards shewed any Reluctance to act as Principals, were never Trusted, always Suspected, and often severely Beaten, and some of them were many ways inhumanly Treated, and that particularly by Williams, the Lieutenant, who was, in his Nature, a merciless, cruel, and inexorable Wretch, as we shall have occasion to take Notice of again in its Place.

They were now in a new Circumstance of Life, and acting upon a different Stage of Business, tho' upon the same stage as to the Element, the Water; before, they were a Merchant Ship, loaden, upon a good Account, with Merchant Goods from the Coast of Barbary, and bound to the Coast of Italy: But they were now a Crew of Pirates, or as they call them in the Levant, Corsaires, Bound no where, but to look out for Purchase and Spoil wherever they could find it.

In persuit of this wicked Trade, they first chang'd the Name of the Ship, which was before call'd the George Gally, and which they call now the Revenge, a Name indeed suitable to the bloody steps they had taken. In the next place they made the best of the Ship's Forces. The Ship had but twelve Guns mounted when they came out of Holland; but as they had six more good Guns in the Hold, with Carriages and every Thing proper for Service, which they had in Store, because being Freighted for the Dutch Merchants, and the Algerines being at War with the Dutch, they suppos'd they might want them for Defence. Now they took care to Mount them for a much worse Design; so that now they had 18 Guns, tho' too many for the number of Hands they had on Board.

In the third Place, instead of persuing their Voyage to Genoa with the Ship's Cargo, they took a clear contrary

Course, and resolv'd to station themselves upon the Coasts of Spain and Portugal, and to cruise upon all Nations; but what they chiefly aim'd at was a Ship with Wine, if possible, for that they wanted Extreamly.

The first Prize they took was an English Sloop, belonging to Pool, Thomas Wise, Commander, bound from Newfoundland with Fish, for Cadiz. This was a Prize of no Value to them, for they knew not what to do with the Fish; so they took out the Master, Mr Wise, and his Men, who were but Five in Number, with their Anchors, and Cables, and Sails, and what else they found worth taking out, and sunk the Vessel.

N.B, Here it is to be observ'd, they found a Man very fit for their Turn, one James Belvin; he was Boatswain of the Sloop, a stout, brisk Fellow, and a very good Sailor; but otherways wicked enough to suit with their Occasion, and as soon as he came among them, he discover'd it; for tho' he was not in the first bloody Contrivance, nor in the terrible execution of which I have given a Relation, that is to say, he was not guilty of running away with the Ship, George Gally, nor of murthering the four innocent Men, which we have given an Account of above; yet, 'tis evident he joyn'd Heartily in all the Villanies which follow'd. And, indeed, this Man's Fate is a just and needful Caution to all those Sailors, who, being taken in other Ships by the

Pirates, think that is a sufficient Plea for them to act as real Pirates afterwards; and that the Plea, or Pretence of being forced, will be a sufficient Protection to them, however Guilty they may have been afterward, and however Volunteir they may have Acted when they come among the Pirates.

Doubtless 'tis possible for a man to prove a hearty Rogue after he is forced into the Service of the Pirates, however Honest he was before, and however Undesignedly or against his Consent he at first come among them. Therefore those who expect to be Acquitted in a Court of Justice afterward, on Pretence of their being at first forced into the Company of Rogues, must take care not to act any thing in Concert with them, while they are Embark'd together, but what they really cannot Avoid, and are apparently under a constraint in the doing.

But this Man, 'twas plain, acted a quite different Part; for after he took on with them, he took all Occasions to engage their Confidence, and to convince them that he was hearty in his joyning them. In a Word, he was the most active and vigorous Fellow of any that were, as it may be said, forced into their Service; for many of the others, tho' they acted with them, and were apparently Assisting, yet there was always a kind of Backwardness and Disgust at the Villainy, for which they were often maltreated, and always suspected by their Masters.

The next Prize they took was a Scotch Vessel, bound from Glasgow, with Herrings and Salmon, from thence to Genoa, and commanded by one Mr John Somerville, of Port Patrick; this Vessel was likewise of very little Value to them, except that they took out, as they had done from the other, their Arms, Ammunition, Cloths, Provisions, Sails, Anchors, Cables, &c., and every Thing of Value, and therefore they sunk her too, as they had done the Sloop. The Reason they gave for sinking these two Vessels was, to prevent their being Discover'd; for, as they were now Cruising on the Coast of Portugal, had they let the Ships have gone with several of their Men on Board, they would presently have stood in for the Shore, and have given the Alarm; and the Men of War, of which there were several, as well Dutch as English, in the River of Lisbon, would presently have put out to Sea in Quest of them. And they were very unwilling to leave the Coast of Portugal, till they had got a Ship with Wine, which they very much wanted.

They Cruised eight or ten days after this, without seeing so much as one Vessel upon the Seas, and were just resolving to stand more to the Norward, to the Coast of Gallitia, when they descryed a Sail to the Southward, being a Ship about as big as their own. tho' they could not perceive what Force she had; however, they gave Chase, and the Vessel perceiving it, crowded from them with all the

Sail they could make, hoisting up French Colours, and standing away to the Southward.

They continued the Chase three Days and three Nights; and tho' they did not gain much upon her, the Frenchman sailing very well, yet they kept her in sight all the while, and for the most part within Gunshot. But the third Night, the Weather proving a little Haizy, the Frenchman chang'd his Course in the Night, and so got clear of them, and good reason they had to bless themselves in the Escape they had made: If they had but known what a dreadful crew of Rogues they had fallen among, if they had been taken.

They were now gotten a long way to the Southward, and being greatly Disappointed, and in want of Water, as well as Wine, they resolved to stand away for the Maderas, which they knew was not far off, so they accordingly made the Island in two Days more; and keeping a large Offing, they cruis'd for three or four Days more, expecting to meet with some Portuguese Vessel going in or coming out; but 'twas in vain, for nothing stirr'd. So, tir'd with Expecting, they stood in for the Road, and came to an Anchor, tho' at a great Distance; then they sent their Boat towards the Shore with seven Men, all well Arm'd, to see whether it might not be Practicable to Board one of the Ships in the Road, and, cutting her away from her Anchors, bring her off; or, if they found that could not be done, then their

Orders were to Intercept some of the Boats, belonging to the Place, which carry Wines off on Board the Ships in the Road, or from one Place to another on the Coast; but they came back again disappointed in both; every Body being alarm'd and aware of them, knowing by their Posture what they were.

Having thus spent several days to no Purpose, and finding themselves Discovered (at length being apparently under the Necessity to make an Attempt some where), they stood away for Porto Santa, about ten Leagues to the Windward of Maderas, and belonging also to the Portuguese; here putting up British Colours, they sent their Boat ashore with Captain Somerville's Bill of Health, and a Present to the Governor of three Barrels of Salmon, and six Barrels of Herrings, and a very civil Message, desiring leave to Water, and to buy some Refreshments, pretending to be Bound to ----

The Governor very courteously granted their Desire; but with more Courtesie than Discretion, went off himself, with about nine or ten of his principal people, to pay the English Captain a visit, little thinking what a kind of a Captain it was they were going to Compliment, and what price it might have cost them.

However, Gow, handsomely dress'd, received them with some ceremony, and entertain'd them tollerably well for a while; but the Governor having been kept by Civillity as they could, and the Refreshments from the Shore not appearing, he was forced to Unmask; and when the Governor and his Company rose up to take their leave, they were, to their great surprise, suddenly surrounded with a gang of Fellows with Musquets and an Officer at the Head of them, who told them, in so many words, they were the Captain's Prisoners, and must not think of going on shore any more, till the water and Provisions, which were promised, should come on Board.

It is impossible to conceive the Consternation and Surprize the Portuguese Gentry were in; nor is it very Decently to be express'd; the poor Governor was so much more than half-dead with the Fright, that he really Befoul'd himself in a piteous Manner, and the rest were in no much better Condition; they trembl'd, cry'd, begg'd, cross'd themselves, and said their Prayers as Men going to Execution; but 'twas all one; they were told flatly the Captain was not to be Trifled with, that the Ship was in want of Provisions, and they would have them, or they would carry them all away. They were, however, well enough treated, except the Restraint of their Persons, and were often ask'd to Refresh themselves, but they would neither Eat or Drink any more all the while they stay'd on Board, which was till the next Day in the Evening, when to their great Satisfaction they saw a great Boat come off from the Fort, and which came directly on Board with seven Buts of Water, and a Cow and a Calf, and a good number of Fowls.

When the Boat came on Board, and had delivered the Stores, Captain Gow complimented the Governour and his Gentlemen, and Discharg'd them to their great Joy; and besides Discharging them, he gave them, in return for the Provisions they brought, two Cerons of Bees Wax, and fir'd them three Guns at their going away. I suppose, however, they will have a care how they go on Board of any Ship again in Compliment to their Captain, unless they are very sure who they are.

Having had no better Success in this out of the way run, to the Maderas, they resolved to make the best of their way back again to the Coast of Spain or Portugal; they accordingly left Porto Santa the next Morning, with a fair Wind, standing directly for Cape St Vincent, or the Southward Cape.

They had not been upon the Coast of Spain above two or three Days, before they met with a New England Ship, ----- Cross, Commander, laden with staves, and bound for Lisbon, and being to Load there with Wine for London; this was a Prize also of no Value to them, and they began to be very much discouraged with their bad Fortune. However, they took out Captain Cross and his men, which were seven or eight in Number, with most of the Provisions and some of the Sails, and gave the Ship to Captain Wise, the Poor Man who they took at first in a Sloop from New-foundland; and in order to pay Wise and his Men for what he took from them, and made them satisfaction, as he call'd it, he gave to Captain Wise and his Mate 24 Cerons of Bees Wax, and to each of his Men, who were four in Number, two Cerons of Wax each; thus he pretended Honestly, and to make Reperation of Damages by giving them the Goods which he had robb'd the Dutch Merchants of, whose Super-Cargo he had Murdered.

After this, Cruising some Days off the Bay, they met with a French Ship from Cadiz, laden with Wine, Oyl, and Fruit; this was in some respect the very Thing they wanted; so they mann'd her with their own men, and stood off to Sea, that they might divide the spoil of her with more Safety, for they were too near the Land.

And first they took out the French Master and all his Men, which were twelve in Number; then they shifted great Part of the Cargo, especially of the Wine, with some Oyl, and a large quantity of Almonds, out of the French Ship into their own; with five of his best Guns, and their Carriages, all their Ammunition and small Arms, and all the best of their Sails, and then he gave that ship to Captain Somerville, the Glasgow Captain, whose ship they had sunk, and to Captain Cross, the New England Captain, who they had taken but just before; and to do Justice, as they call'd it, here also, they gave half the Ship and Cargo to Somerville, one quarter to his Mate, and the other quarter to Capt. Cross, and 16 Cerons of Wax to the Men to be shar'd among them.

It is to be observ'd here, that Captain Somerville carryed all his Men along with him; except one who chose to enter among the Pirates, so that he could never pretend he was forced into their service; but Cross's Men were all detain'd, whether by Force, or by their own Consent, does not appear at present.

The Day before this Division of the Spoil, they saw a large Ship to Windward, which at first put them into some Surprise, for she came bearing down directly upon them, and they thought she had been a Portuguese Man-of-War, but they found soon after that it was a Merchant Ship, had French Colours, and bound Home, as they suppos'd, from the West Indies, and it was so; for, as we afterwards learn'd, she was loaden at Martinico, and bound for Rochelle.

The Frenchman, not fearing them, came on large to the Wind, being a Ship of much greater Force than Gow's Ship, and carrying 32 Guns and 80 Men, besides a great many Passengers; however, Gow at first made as if he would lye by for them, but seeing plainly what a Ship it was, and that they should have their Hands full of her, he began to consider, and calling his Men all together upon the Deck, told them his Mind---viz., That the Frenchman was apparently superior in Force every way, that they were but ill mann'd, and had a great many Prisoners on Board, and that some of their own People were not very well to be trusted, that six of their best Hands were on Board the Prize, and that all they had left were not sufficient to ply their Guns and stand by the Sails; and that therefore, as they were under no Necessity to engage, so he thought it would be next to Madness to think of it, the French Ship being so very much Superior to them in Force.

The generality of the Men were of Gow's Mind, and agreed to decline the Fight, but Williams, his Lieut., strenuously oppos'd it, and being not to be appeas'd by all that Gow could say to him, or any one else, flew out in a Rage at Gow, upbraiding him with being a Coward, and not fit to command a Ship of Force.

The Truth is, Gow's Reasoning was Good, and the Thing was Just, considering their own Condition. But Williams was a Fellow uncapable of any solid Thinking, had a kind of a savage, brutal Courage, but nothing of true Bravery in him; and this made him the most desperate and outrageous Villain in the World, and the most cruel and inhumane to those whose Disaster it was to fall into his Hands, as had frequently appear'd in his Usage of the Prisoners, under his Power, in this very Voyage.

Gow was a man of Temper, and notwithstanding all the ill Language Williams gave him, said little or nothing, but by way of Argument, against attacking the French Ship, which would certainly have been too strong for them. But this provok'd Williams the more; and he grew to such an extravagant height, that he demanded boldly of Gow to give his Orders For Fighting, which Gow declined still, Williams presented his Pistol at him, and snapt it, but it did not go off, which enrag'd him the more.

Winter and Peterson standing nearest to Williams, and seeing him so furious, flew at him immediately, and each of them fir'd a Pistol at him, one shot him thro' the Arm, and the other into his Belly, at which he fell, and the men about him laid hold of him to throw him Overboard, believing he was dead; but as they lifted him up, he started violently out of their Hands, and leaped directly into the Hold, and from thence run desperately into the Powder-Room, with his Pistol cock'd in his Hand, swearing he would blow them all up; and had certainly done it, if they had not seiz'd him just as he had gotten the Scuttle open, and was that Moment going in to put his hellish Resolution in practice.

Having thus secur'd the demented raving Creature, they carryed him forward to the Place which they had made on Purpose, between Decks, to secure their Prisoners, and put him in amongst them, having first loaded him with Irons, and particularly Hand-cuffed him with his Hands behind him, to the great satisfaction of the other Prisoners, who knowing what a butcherly, furious Fellow he was, were terrified, to the last Degree, to see him come in among them; till they saw the Condition he came in. He was, indeed, the Terror of all the Prisoners, for he usually treated them in a barbarous manner, without the least Provocation, and merely for his Humour; presenting Pistols to their Breasts, swearing he would shoot them that Moment, and then would beat them unmercifully, and all for his Diversion, as he call'd it.

Having thus laid him fast, they presently resolv'd to stand away to the Westward, by which they quitted the Martinico Ship, who by that time was come nearer to them, and farther convinc'd them they were in no Condition to have Engag'd her, for she was a stout Ship and full of Men.

All this happen'd Just the Day before they shar'd their last Prize among the Prisoners (as I have said), in which they put on such a Mock-face of doing Justice to the several Captains and Mates, and other Men, their Prisoners, whose

Ships they had taken away, and who now they made a Reparation to, by giving then what they had taken Violently from another, that it was a strange Medly of Mock-Justice made up of Rapine and Generosity blended together.

Two Days after this they took a Bristol Ship, bound from Newfoundland to Oporto with Fish; they let her Cargo alone, for they had no occasion for Fish, but they took out also almost all their Provisions, all the Ammunition, Arms, &c., all her good Sails, also her best Cables, and forced two of her Men to go away with them, and then put 10 of the French Men on Board her, and let her go.

But just as they were parting with her, they consulted together what to do with Williams, their Lieutenant, who was then among their Prisoners, and in Irons; and after a short Debate, they resolved to put him on Board the Bristol Man and send him away too, which accordingly was done; with Directions to the Master to deliver him on Board the first English Man of War, they should meet with, in order to his being hang'd for a Pirate (so they jeeringly call'd him) as soon as he came to England, giving them also an Account of some of his Villanies.

The Truth is, this Williams was a Monster, rather than a Man; he was the most inhuman, bloody, and desperate Creature that the World could produce; he was even too wicked for Gow and all his crew, tho' they were Pirates and Murtherers, as has been said; his Temper was so Savage, so Villainous, so Merciless, that even the Pirates themselves told him it was Time he was hang'd out of the Way.

One Instance of this Barbarity in Williams can not be omitted, and will be sufficient to justify all that can be said of him, namely, that when Gow gave it as a Reason against engaging with the Martinico Ship, that he had a great many Prisoners on Board (as above), and some of their own Men they could not depend upon; Williams propos'd to have them all call'd up, one by one, and to cut their Throats, and throw them Overboard; A Proposal so Horrid, that the worst of the Crew shook their Heads at it; yet Gow answer'd him very handsomly, That there had been too much Blood spilt already; yet the refusing this highten'd the Quarrel, and was the chief Occasion of his offering to Pistol Gow himself, as has been said at large. After which, his Behaviour was such as made all the Ship's Crew resolve to be rid of him. And 'twas thought, if they had not had an Opportunity to send him away, as they did by the Bristol Ship, they would have been oblig'd to have hang'd him themselves.

This cruel and butcherly Temper of Williams being carry'd to such a height, so near to the ruine of them all, shock'd some of them, and as they acknowledg'd gave them some check in the heat of their wicked Progress, and had they had a fair Opportunity to have gone on Shore at the Time, without falling into the Hands of Justice, 'tis believ'd the greatest Part of them would have abandon'd the Ship, and perhaps the very Trade of a Pirate too. But they had dipt their Hands in Blood, and Heaven had no doubt determin'd to bring them, that is to say, the Chief of them, to the Gallows for it, as indeed they all deserv'd, so they went on.

When they put Williams on board the Bristol Man, and he was told what Directions they gave with him, he began to resent, and made all the Intercession he could to Captain Gow for Pardon, or at least not to be put on board the Ship, knowing if he was carried to Lisbon, he should meet with his Due from the Portuguese, if not from the English; for it seems he had been concern'd in some Villanies among the Portuguese, before he came on Board the George Galley; what they were he did not confess, nor indeed did his own Ship's Crew trouble themselves to examine him about it. He had been wicked enough among them, and it was sufficient to make them use him as they did; it was more to be wonder'd, indeed, they did not cut him in pieces upon the Spot, and throw him into the Sea, half on one side of the Ship, and half on the other; for there was scarce a Man in the Ship, but on one Occasion or other, had some apprehensions of him, and might be said to go in danger of his life from him.

But they chose to shift their Hands of him this bloodless way; so they double fetter'd him and brought him up. When they brought him out among the Men, he begg'd they would throw him into the Sea and drown him; then entreated for his Life with a meanness which made them despise him, and with Tears, so that one Time they began to relent; but then the devilish Temper of the Fellow overrul'd it again; so at last they resolv'd to let him go, and did accordingly put him on Board, and gave him a hearty Curse at parting, wishing him a good Voyage to the Gallows, as was made good afterwards, tho' in such Company as they little thought of at that Time.

The Bristol Captain was very just to them, for according to their Orders, as soon as they came to Lisbon, they put him on board the Argyle, one of His Majesty's Ships, Captain Bowler, Commander, then lying in the Tagus, and bound Home for England, who accordingly brought him Home; tho', as it happen'd, Heaven brought the Captain and the rest of the Crew so quickly to the end of their Villanies, that they all came Home time enough to be hang'd with their Lieutenant. But I return to Gow and his Crew. Having thus dismiss'd the Bristol Man, and clear'd his Hands of most of his Prisoners, he, with the same wicked Generosity, gave the Bristol Captain 13 Cerons of Bees Wax, as a Gratuity for his Trouble and Charge with the Prisoners, and in Recompense, as he call'd it, for the Goods he had taken from him, and so they parted.

What these several Captains did, to whom they thus divided the spoil of poor Ferneau's Cargo, or as I ought rather to call it, of the Merchants Cargo, which was loaded in Africa; I say, what was done with the Bees-Wax, and other Things which they distributed to the Captains, and their Crews, who they thus transpos'd from Ship to Ship, that we cannot tell, nor indeed could these people either well know how to keep it, or how to part with it.

It was certainly a Gift they had no power to give, nor had the other any Right to it by their Donation; but as the Owners were unknown, and the several Persons possessing it are not easily known, I do not see which way the poor Dutchmen can come at their Goods again.

It is true, indeed, the Ships which they exchang'd may, and ought to be restored, and the honest Owners put in Possession of them again, and I suppose will be so in a legal Manner; but the Goods were so dispers'd that it was impossible.

This was the last Prize they took, not only on the Coast of Portugal, but any where else; for Gow who, to give him his due, was a Fellow of Council, and had a great Presence of Mind in Cases of Exigence, consider'd that as soon as the Bristol Ship came into the River of Lisbon, they would certainly give an Account of them, as well of their strength, as of their Station in which they Cruized; and that consequently the English Men of War, of which there are generally some in that River, would immediately come Abroad to look for them. So he began to Reason with his Officers, that now the Coast of Portugal would be no proper Place at all for them, unless they resolved to fall into the Hand of the said Men of War; and that they ought to consider immediately what to do.

In these Debates, some advised one Thing, some another, as is usual in like Cases; some were for going on to the Coast of Guinea, where (as they said) was Purchase enough, and very rich Ships to be taken; others were for going to the West Indies, and to Cruise among the Islands, and take up their Station at Tobago; others, and that not those of the most Ignorant, propos'd the standing in to the Bay of Mexico, and to joyn in with some of a new sort of Pirates at St Jago de la Cuba, who are all Spaniards, and call themselves Garda del Coasta, that is, Guardships for the Coast; but under that pretence make Prize of Ships of all Nations, and sometimes even of their own Countrymen too, but especially of the English; but when this was propos'd it was answered, they durst not trust the Spaniards.

Another sort was for going to the North of America, and after having taken a Sloop or two on the Coast of New-England or New-York, laden with Provisions for the West-Indies, which would not have been very hard to do, such being often passing and re-passing there, and by which they might have been sufficiently stor'd with Provision, then to have gone away to the South Seas; but Gow objected, that they were not Mann'd sufficiently for such an Undertaking; and likewise, that they had not sufficient Stores of Ammunition, especially of Powder, and of small Arms for any considerable Action with the Spaniards.

Then it was offered by the Boatswain, who it seems had been in that Part of the World, to go away to the Honduras, and to the Bay of Campeachy among the Buccaniers and Logwood Cutters, and there they should in the first Place be sure to pick up forty or fifty stout Fellows, good Sailors, and bold, enterprizing Men, who understand the Spaniards, and the Spanish Coast on both sides of America, as well as any Men in the World, and had all Fire Arms with them, and Ammunition too, and that being well Mann'd, they might take their hazard for Provisions, which might be had any where, at least of one Sort if not another; besides, when they were thoroughly Mann'd, they might

Cruise for Provisions any where, and might be as likely to meet with the New-York and New-England Sloops, on the back of the Islands, in their Way to Barbadoes and Jamaica as any where.

Others said they should go first to the Islands of New-Providence, or to the Mouth of the Gulph of Florida, and then cruising on the coast of North-America, and making their Retreat at New Providence, Cruize from the Gulf of Florida, North upon the Coast of Carolina, and as high as the Capes of Virigina. But nothing could be resolv'd on; till at last Gow let them into the Secret of a Project, which, as he told them, he had long had in his Thoughts; and which was, to go away to the North of Scotland, near the Coast of which, as he said, he was Born and Bred; and where he said, if they met with no Purchase upon the Sea, he could tell them how they should Enrich themselves by going on Shore.

To bring them to concur with this Design, he represented the Danger they were in, where they were (as above): The Want they were in of Fresh Water, and of several kinds of Provisions, but above all, the necessity they were in of careening and cleaning their Ship: That it was too long a run for them to go to the Southward; and that they had not Provisions to serve them till they could reach to any Place Proper for that Purpose; and might be driven to the utmost Distress, if they should be put by from Watering, either by Weather or Enemies.

Also he told them, if any of the Men of War came out in search of them, they would never Imagine they were gone away to the Northward; so that their Run that Way was perfectly Secure. And he could assure them of his own Knowledge, that if they landed in such places as he should direct, they could not fail of a comfortable Booty in Plundering some Gentlemen's Houses, who liv'd Secure and Unguarded very near the Shore. And that tho' the Country should be Alarmed, yet before the Government could send any Men of War to Attack them, they might clear their Ship, lay in a Store of Fresh Provisions, and be gone; and besides that, they would get a good many stout Fellows to go along with them, upon his Encouragement; and that they should be better Mann'd than they were yet, and should be Ready against all Events.

These Arguments, and their approaching Fate concurring, had a sufficient Influence on the Ship's Company to prevail on them to Consent. So they made the best of their Way to the Northward, and about the middle of last January they arriv'd at Carristoun, in the Isles of Orkney, and came to an Anchor in a Place which Gow told them was safe Riding, under the Lee of a small Island at some Distance from the Port.

Gow being Sole Director, as well as Commander of the Ship, call'd them all together, to tell them what Account they should give of themselves, when they came to Converse with any of the People of the Island, that they might agree in their Story, and give no cause of Suspicion; and 'tis most certain, that had they been careful to observe his Directions, and not betray'd and Expos'd themselvs, they might have pass'd undiscover'd, and done all the Mischief they intended, without allarming the Country. His Orders were, that they should say they came from Cadiz, and were bound for Stockholm, and thence to Dantzick; but that they had had a long Passage, by reason of contrary Winds, and lost their Opportunity of passing the Sound, which was now full of Ice, if not frozen up; and that they had been driven so far to the Northward, by stress of Weather, that they wanted Water and fresh Provisions, and to clean their Ship; that they would pay for whatever they were supply'd with; and that by the Time they had clean'd their Ship, they hoped the Weather would be Warm, and the Seas open for them to proceed on their Voyage. This Tale was easie to tell, and probable enough, and therefore likely enough to be believed; and they all oblig'd themselves to give the same Account exactly, and not to vary the least Tittle of it, or so much as Whisper otherwise, upon Pain of Immediate Death.

In Carristown Harbour they found a small Scotch Bark, – Lumsdale, Master, loaden with Wine and Brandy, and bound about to the Isle of Man. This was a welcome thing to them all; and had it been any where else, they would have made it a good Prize. But as they had Goods sufficient on Board, and such as were very acceptable Merchandise, Lumsdale traded freely with them, and Gow bartered seven Cerons of Wax, and about 200l. weight of Barbary Copper with him for a Hogshead of Geneva and an Anchor of Brandy, and some other Goods; and it was believed that Gow had some Money into the Bargain.

A day or two after, a Swedish Vessel came into the Road, bound from Stockholm to Glasgow, and laden with Swedes Iron, and East Country Plants; they traded with her also for 20 Coil of new Rope, for which Gow gave the Master eleven Ceron of Bees Wax. It has been said, they plundered this Vessel of several other Goods, and oblig'd the Master to promise to Sail directly to his Port, without speaking to any body, on pain of sinking the Ship. But this wants Confirmation; nor is it probable they would venture to do so in a Port where they resolved to stay any long time, and where they knew it was so necessary to be entirely conceal'd.

But now their Misfortunes began to come on, and Things look'd but with an indifferent aspect upon them;

for several of their Men, especially such of them as had been forc'd or decoy'd into their Service, began to think of making their Escape from them; and to cast about for means to bring it to pass. The first was a young Man, who was originally one of the Ship's Company, but was Forced by fear of being Murther'd, as has been observ'd, to give a silent Assent to go with them, he took an Opportunity to get away.

It was one Evening when the Boat went on Shore (for they kept a civil Correspondence with the People of the Town), this young Fellow being one of the Ship's Crew, and having been several Times on Shore before, and therefore not suspected, gave them the Slip, and got away to a Farm-house which lay under a Hill, out of sight; and there, for two or three Pieces of Eight, he got a Horse, and soon, by that means, escap'd to Kirkwall, a Market-Town, and the chief of the Orkneys, about 12 Miles from the Place where the Ship lay.

As soon as he came there, he surrender'd himself to the Government, desiring Protection, and inform'd them who Gow was, and what the Ship's Crew were, and upon what Business they were Abroad; with what else he knew of their Designs, as to Plundering the Gentlemens' Houses, &c., upon which they immediately rais'd the Country, and got a strength together to defend themselves.

But the next Disaster that attended them, was (for misfortunes seldom come alone) more fatal than this, for 10 of Gow's Men, most of them likewise Men forced into the Service, went away with the long Boat, making the best of their Way for the main Land of Scotland.

N.B. These Men, however they did, and what shift soever they made to get so far, were taken in the Firth of Edenburg, and made Prisoners there.

Had Gow taken the Alarm, as he ought to have done, at either of these Accidents, and put to Sea, either stood over for the Coast of Norway, or have run thro' Westward, between the Islands, and gone for the Isle of Man, or for the North of Ireland, he might easily have gone clear off; for there was no Vessel in the Country that was of Force sufficient to have spoken with him.

But harden'd for his own Destruction, and Justice evidently pursuing him, he grew the Bolder for the Disaster; and notwithstanding that the Country was alarm'd, and that he was fully discover'd, instead of making a timely Escape, he resolved to land upon them, and to put his intended Projects, (viz.) of Plundering the Gentlemens' Houses, in Execution, whatever it cost him.

In Order to this, he sent the Boatswain and 10 Men on Shore the very same Night, very well Arm'd, directing them to go to the House of Mr Honnyman of Grahamsey,

Sheriff of the County, and who was himself at that Time to his great good Fortune, from Home. The People of the House had not the least Notice of their coming, so that when they knock'd at the Door, it was immediately open'd; upon when they all enter'd the House at once, except one Panton, who they set Centinel, and order'd him to stand at the Door to secure their Retreat, and to secure any from coming in after them.

Mrs Honnyman and her Daughter were extreamly Frighted at the sight of so many Armed Men coming into the House, and ran screaming about like People Distracted, while the Pirates, not regarding them, were looking about for Chests and Trunks, where they might expect to find some Plunder. And Mrs Honnyman, in her Fright, coming to the Door, ask'd Panton, the Man who was set Centinel there, what the meaning of it all was? and he told her freely, they were Pirates, and that they came to Plunder the House. At this she recovered some Courage, and run back into the House immediately; and knowing, to be sure, where her Money lay, which was very considerable, and all in Gold, she put the Bags in her Lap, and boldly rushing by Panton, who thought she was only running from them, in a Fright, carryed it all off, and so made her Escape with the Treasure. The Boatswain being inform'd that the Money was carryed off, resolved to revenge himself by burning the Writings and Papers, which they call there the Charter of their Estates, and are always of great Value in Gentlemen's Houses of Estates; but the young Lady, Mr Honeyman's Daughter, hearing them threaten to burn the Writings, watch'd her Opporttunity, and running to the Charter Room where they lay, and tying the most considerable of them up in a Napkin, threw them out of the Window, jumpt after them herself, and Escaped without Damage; tho' the Window was one Story high at least.

However, the Pirates had the Plundering of all the rest of the House, and carried off a great deal of Plate and Things of Value; and forced once of the Servants, who played very well on the Bagpipe, to march along, Piping before them, when they carryed them off to the Ship.

The next Day they weigh'd Anchor, intending, tho' they had clean'd but one side of the Ship, to put out to Sea and quit the Coast; but sailing Eastward, they came to an Anchor again, at a little Island, call'd Calfsound; and, having some farther Mischief in their view here, the Boat-swain went on Shore again, with some Armed Men; but meeting with no other Plunder, they carryed off three Women, who they kept on Board some time, and used so Inhumanly, that when they set them on Shore again, they were not able to go or to stand; and we hear that one of them dyed on the Beach where they left them.

The next Day they weigh'd again, holding the same Course Eastward, thro' the Openings between the Islands, till they came off of Rossness. And now Gow resolved to make the best of his Way for the Island of Eda, to Plunder the House of Mr Fea, a Gentleman of a considerable Estate, and who Gow had some Acquaintance with, having been at School together when they were youths.

It seems Gow's Reason for resolving to attack this Gentleman, who was his old Acquaintance, was that he thought the Alarm, given at Carristown, would necessarily draw the Gentlemen, and the best of their Forces, that Way; which Guess was far from being Improbable; for just so it was, only with Respect to Mr Fea, who having had the Allarm with the rest, yet stay'd at Home, on a particular Occasion, his Wife being, at that Time, very much Indisposed.

It is to be observ'd here that Carristoun and Eda lye with Respect to each other (N. East and S. West), and the Bodies of the Chief Islands lye between them.

On the 13th of February, in the Morning, Gow appearing with his Ship off the Island, call'd the Calfsound, Mr Fea and his Family were very much alarm'd, not being able to gather above six or seven Men for his Defence; he therefore wrote a Letter to Gow, intending to send it on Board, as soon as he should get into the Harbour, to desire him to forbear the usual Salutes with his great Guns; because Mrs Fea, his Wife, was so very much Indispos'd. And this, as he would oblige his old School-fellow, telling him, at the same time, that the Inhabitants were all fled to the Mountain, on the Report of his being a Pirate, which he hoped would not prove true; in which Case, he should be very ready to supply him with all such Necessaries as the Island would afford; desiring him to send the Messenger safe back, at whose Return the Allarms of the People would immediately be at an End.

The Tide, it seems, runs extreamly Rapid among those Islands, and the Navigation is thereby render'd very dangerous and uncertain. Gow was an able Seaman; but he was no Pilot for that Place, and which was worse, he had no Boat to Assist, in case of Extremity, to ware the Ship; and in turning into Calf Sound, he stood a little too near the Point of a little Island, call'd the Calf, and which lay in the middle of the Passage; here his Ship, missing stays, was in great Danger of going ashore; to avoid which he drop'd an Anchor under his Foot, which taking good hold, brought him up, and he thought the Danger was over.

But as the Wind was, he lay so near the shore that he could not get under Sail again, for want of a Boat to Tow him out of the Channel, or to carry off an Anchor to heave him out.

That little Island above is uninhabited, but affords Pasture to five or six Hundred Sheep, which Mr Fea always keeps upon it, for it belonged wholly to him. Gow was now in Distress, and had no Remedy but to send his small Boat on shore to Mr Fea, to desire his Assistance – that is to say, to desire him to lend him a Boat to carry out an Anchor to heave off the Ship.

Mr Fea sent back the Boat with one, James Laing, in it, with the Letter, which I have already mentioned; Gow sent him back immediately with this Answer, by Word of Mouth – viz., that he could write to no Body. But if Mr Fea would order his People to assist him with a Boat, to carry out an Anchor, he would Reward them handsomly. Mr Fea, in the mean time, ordered his great Boat (for he had such a Boat as Gow wanted) to be stav'd and launch'd into the Water and sunk, and the Masts, Sails, and Oars to be carryed privately out of Sight.

While this was doing Mr Fea perceiv'd Gow's Boat coming on Shore, with five Persons in her. These Men having landed on the main Island, left their Boat on the Beach, and all together march'd directly up to the Mansion House. This put him into some Surprize at first. However, he resolv'd to meet them in a peaceable manner, tho' he perceiv'd they were all double Arm'd; when he came up to them he entreated them not to go up to the House, because of the languishing Condition of his Wife; that she was already frighted with the Rumours which had been rais'd of their being Pirates, and that she would certainly die with the fear she was in for herself and Family, if they came to the Door.

The Boatswain answer'd, they did not desire to fright his Wife, or any Body else; but they came to desire the assistance of his Boat, and if he would not grant them so small a Favour, he had nothing to expect from them but the utmost Extremity. Mr Fea returned that they knew well enough he could not answer giving them, or lending them his Boat, or any help, as they appear'd to be such People as was reported; but that if they would take them by Force, he could not help himself.

But in the mean time, talking still in a friendly Manner to them, he ask'd them to go to a neighbouring House, which he said was a Change House, that is a Publick House, and take a Cup of Ale with him.

This they consented to, seeing Mr Fea was all alone, so they went all with him; Mr Fea in the mean time found means to give private Orders that the Oars, and Mast, and Sails of the Pirates' Boat should be all carry'd away, and that in a quarter of an Hour after they had sat together, he should be call'd hastily out of the Room on some pretence or other of some Body to speak with him, all which was perform'd to a Tittle.

When he had got from them, he gave Orders that his Six Men, who, as before, he had got together, and who were now come to him well arm'd, should place themselves at a certain stile, behind a thick Hedge, and which was about half the way between the Ale-House and his own House; that if he came that way with the Boatswain alone, they should suddenly start out upon them both, and throwing him down, should seize upon the other; but that if all the five came with him, he would take an Occasion to be either before or behind them, so that they might all fire upon them without danger of hurting him.

Having given these Orders, and depending upon their being well executed, he returned to the Company, and having given them more Ale, told them he would gladly do them any service that he could lawfully do, and that if they would take the trouble of walking up to his House in a peaceable Manner, that his Family might not be frighted with seeing himself among them, they should have all the Assistance that was in his Power.

The Fellows, whether they had taken too much Ale, or whether the Condition of their Ship, and the Hopes of getting a Boat to help them, blinded their Eyes, is not certain, fell with ease into his Snare, and agreed readily to go along with Mr Fea; but after a while resolv'd not to go all of them, only deput'd the Boatswain to go, which was what Mr Fea most desir'd. The Boatswain was very willing to accept of the Trust, but it was observ'd he took a great deal of care of his Arms, which was no less than four Pistols, all loaded with a brace of Bullets each; nor would he be persuaded to leave any of them behind him, no not with his own Men.

In this Posture Mr Fea and the Boatswain walk'd along together very quietly till they came to the Stile, which having got over, Mr Fea, seeing his Men all ready, turn'd short about upon the Boatswain, and taking him by the Collar, told him he was his Prisoner, and the same Moment the rest of his Men rushing upon them, threw them both down, and so secur'd the Boatswain without giving him time so much as to fire one Pistol. He cry'd out indeed with all his Might to alarm his Men, but they soon stopt his Mouth, by first forcing a Pistol into it, and then a Handkerchief, and having disarm'd him, and bound his Hands behind him, and his Feet together, Mr Fea left him there under a Guard, and with his five other Men, but without any Arms, at least that could be seen, return'd to the Ale House to the rest. The House having two Doors, they divided themselves, and having rush'd in at both Doors at the same time, they seiz'd all the four Men before they were aware, or had time to lay hold of their Arms. They did indeed what Men could do, and one of them snapp'd a

Pistol at Mr Fea, but it did not go off; and Mr Fea snatching at the Pistol at the same Moment to divert the Shot if it had fir'd, struck his Hand with such force against the Cock, as very much bruised his Hand.

They were all five now in his Power, and he sent them away under a good Guard to a Village in the middle of the Island, where they were kept separate from one another, and sufficiently secur'd.

Then Mr Fea dispatch'd Expresses to the Gentlemen in the neighbouring Islands, to acquaint them with what he had done, and to desire their speedy Assistance; also desiring earnestly that they would take care that no Boat should go within reach of the Pirate's Guns; and at Night he, Mr Fea, caus'd Fires to be made upon the Hill round him, to allarm the Country, and ordered all the Boats round the Island to be haul'd up upon the Beach as far as was possible, and disabled also, least the pirates should swim from the Ship and get any of them into their Possession.

Next Day, the 14th, it blew very hard all Day; and in the Evening, about High Water, it shifted to W.N.W., upon which the Pirates set their Sails, expecting to get off, and so to lay it round the Island, and put out to Sea; but the Fellow who was order'd to cut the Cable check'd the Ship's Way, and consequently, on a sudden, she took all a-back; then the Cable being parted, when it should have held, the

Ship run directly on Shore on the Calf Island; nor could all their Skill prevent it. Then Gow, with an Air of Desperation, told them they were all dead Men. Nor indeed could it be otherways, for having lost the only Boat they had, and five of their best Hands, they were able to do little or nothing towards getting their Ship off; besides, as she went on Shore, on the top of High Water, and a Spring Tide, there was no Hope of getting her off afterward: Wherefore, the next Morning, being Monday the 15th, they hung out a White Flag, as a Signal for Parlee, and sent a man on Shore, upon Calf Island, for now they cou'd go on Shore out of the Ship almost at half Flood.

Now Mr Fea thought he might talk with Gow in a different stile from what he did before, so he wrote a Letter to him, wherein he complain'd of the rude Behaviour of his five Men; for which he told him, he had been oblig'd to seize on them and make them Prisoners; letting him know that the Country, being all allarm'd, would soon be too many for him; and therefore advis'd him to Surrender himself Peacebly, and be the Author of a quiet Surrender of the rest, as the only Means to obtain any Favour; and then he might become an Evidence against the rest, and so might save his own Life.

This Letter Mr Fea sent by a Boat with four armed Men to the Island, to be given to the Fellow that Gow had sent on Shore, and who waited there; and he at the same time gave them a Letter from Gow to Mr Fea; for now he was humble enough to Write, which before he refused.

Gow's Letter to Mr Fea was to let him have some Men and Boats to take out the best of the Cargo, in order to lighten the Ship and set her afloat; and offering himself to come on Shore and be Hostage, for the Security of the Men and Boats, and to give Mr Fea a Thousand Pounds in Goods for the Service: Declaring at the same time, if this small Succour was refus'd him, he would take care no Body should better himself by his Misfortune; for that rather than to be taken, they would set fire to the Ship, and would all Perish together.

Mr Fea reply'd to this Letter, that he had a Boat indeed, that would have been fit for his Service, but that she was stav'd and sunk; but if he would come on Shore quietly without Arms, and bring his Carpenter with him to repair the Boat, he might have her.

This Mr Fea did to give Gow an opportunity to embrace his first offer of Surrendering. But Gow was neither Humble enough to come in, nor Sincere enough to treat with him fairly, if he had intended to let him have the Boat; and if he had, 'tis propable that the former Letter had made the Men Suspicious of him; so that now he could do nothing without communicating it to the rest of the Crew.

About four in the Afternoon Mr Fea received an Answer to his last Letter: The Copy of which is exactly as follows:-

---

"FROM ON BOARD OUR SHIP THE REVENGE, Feb. 16, 1725.

"*HONOUR'D SIR,*

"*I am sorry to hear of the irregular Proceedings of my Men. I gave no Orders to that Effect. And what hath been wrongfully done to the Country, was contrary to my Inclination. It was my Misfortune to be in this Condition at Present. It was in your Power to have done otherwise, in making my Fortune better. Since my being in the Country I have wrong'd no Man, nor taken any Thing, but what I have paid for. My Design in coming was to make the Country the better, which I am still capable to do, providing you are just to me. I thank you for the Concern you have had for my bad Fortune, and am sorry I cannot embrace your Proposal, as being Evidence; my People have already made use of that Advantage. I have by my last signified my Design of Proceeding, provided I can procure no better Terms. Please to send James Laing on Board to continue till my return. I should be glad to have the good Fortune to commune with you upon that subject. I beg you will assist me with a Boat; and be assured I do no Man Harm, wer't it my Power, as I am now at your Mercy. I cannot surrender myself Prisoner; I'd rather commit myself to the Mercy of the Seas: So that if you will incline to contribute to my Escape, shall leave you Ship and Cargo as your Disposal.*

"*I continue, Honoured Sir, &c.,*
"*JOHN SMITH.*"

Upon this Letter, and especially that Part wherein Gow desires to commune with him, Mr Fea believing he might do some service in persuading him to submit, went over to Calf Island, and went on Shore alone, ordering his Boat to lie in readiness to take him in again, but not one Man to stir out of her: And calling to Gow, with a Speaking-Trumpet, desir'd him to come on Shore, which the other readily did: But Mr Fea, before he ventur'd, wisely foresaw, that whilst he was alone upon the Island, the Pirates might, unknown to him, get from the Ship by different Ways, and under Cover of Shore, might get behind and surround him; to prevent which, he set a Man upon the top of his own House, which was on the opposite Shore, and over-looked the whole Island, and order'd him to make Signals with his Flag, waving his Flag once for every Man that he saw come on Shore; but it four or more came on Shore, then to keep the Flag waving continually, till he, Mr Fea, should retire.

This Precaution was very needful, for no sooner was Mr Fea advanc'd upon the Island, expecting Gow to come on Shore to meet him; but he saw a Fellow come from the Ship with a white Flag and a Bottle, and a Glass, and a Bundle; then turning to his own House, he saw his Man make the Signals appointed, and that the Man kept the Flag continually waving, upon which he immediately retir'd to his Boat, and he no sooner got into it, but he saw five Fellows running under Shore, with lighted matches and Granadoes in their Hands, to have Intercepted him, but seeing him out of their Reach, they retir'd to the Ship.

After this the Fellow with the white Flag up, and gave Mr Fea two Letters; he would have left the Bundle, which he said, was a present to Mr Fea; and the Bottle, which he said, was a Bottle of Brandy; but Mr Fea would not take them; but told the Fellow his Captain was a treacherous Villain, and he did not doubt but he should see him hang'd; and as to him, the Fellow, he had a great Mind to shoot him; upon which the Fellow took to his Heels, and Mr Fea, being in his Boat, did not think it worth while to Land again to pursue him. This put an End to all Parlee for the present; but had the Pirates succeeded in this Attempt, they would have so far have gained their Point, either they must have been Assisted, or Mr Fea must have been Sacrific'd.

The Two Letters from Gow were one for Mr Fea, and the other for his Wife, the first was much to the same Purpose as the former; only that in this, Gow requested the great Boat with her Masts, and Sails and Oars, with some Provisions, to transport themselves whether they thought fit to go for their own Safety; offering to leave the Ship and Cargo to Mr Fea; and threatning that if the Men of War arriv'd (for Mr Fea had given him Notice that he expected two Men of War), before he was thus assisted, they would set Fire to the Ship, and blow themselves up; so that as they had liv'd, they would all dye together.

The Letter to Mrs Fea was to desire her to Interceed with her Husband; and Pleading that he was their Countryman, and had been her Husband's School-fellow, &c., but no Answer was returned to either of these Letters. On the 17th, in the Morning, contrary to Expectation, Gow himself came on Shore, upon the Calf-Island, unarm'd, except his Sword, and alone, except one Man at a distance, carrying a white Flag, making Signals for a Parlee.

Mr Fea, who by this time had gotten more People about him, immediately sent one, Mr Fea of Whitehall, and a Gentleman of his own Family, with five other Persons, well Armed, over to the Island, with Orders to secure Gow, if it was possible, by any means, either Dead or Alive. When they came on Shore, he proposed that one of them, whose name was Scollary, a Master of a Vessel, should go on Board the Ship, as Hostage for this Gow's Safety; and Scollary consenting, Gow himself conducted him to the Ship's side.

Mr Fea perceiving this from his own House, immediately took another Boat, and went over to the Island himself. And while he was expostulating with his Men, for letting Scollary go for Hostage, Gow return'd; and Mr Fea made no Hessitation, but told him in short he was his Prisoner; at which Gow starting, said, it ought not to be so, since there was a Hostage delivered for him. Mr Fea said he gave no Order for it, and it was what they could not Justify; and since Scollary had ventured without Orders, he must take his Fate, he would run the Venture of it, but advis'd Gow, as he expected good Usage himself, that he would send the Fellow, who carryed his white Flag, back to the Ship, with Orders for them to return Scollary in safety, and to desire Winter and Peterson to come with him.

Gow declin'd giving any such Orders; but the Fellow said he would readily go and fetch them, and did so, and they came along with them. When Gow saw them, he reproached them for being so easily imposed, and order'd them to go back to the Ship immediately. But Mr Fea's Men, who were too strong for them, surrounded them, and took them all. When this was done, they demanded Gow to deliver his Sword, but he said he would rather dye with it in his Hand, and begg'd them to shoot him. But that was deny'd; and Mr Fea's Men disarming him of his Sword, carried him with the other two, into their Boat, and after that to the main Island where Mr Fea liv'd.

Having thus secur'd the Captain, Mr Fea prevailed with him to go to the Shore, over against the Ship, and to call the Gunner and another Man to come on Ashore on Calf-Island, which they did; but they was no sooner there but they also were surrounded by some Men, which Mr Fea had placed out of sight upon the Island for that Purpose. Then they made Gow to call to the Carpenter to come on Shore, still making them believe they should have a Boat, and Mr Fea went over and met him alone; and talking to him, told him they could not repair the Boat without Help, and without Tools, so persuaded him to go back to the Ship, and bring a Hand or two with him and some Tools, some Ockham, Nails, &c. The Carpenter being thus deluded, went back, and brought a Frenchman and another with him, with all Things proper for their Work; all which, as soon as they came on Shore, were likewise seiz'd and secur'd by Mr Fea and his Men.

But there was still a great many Men in the Ship, who it was necessary to bring, if possible, to a quiet Surrender. So Mr Fea order'd his Men to make a Feint, as if they would go to Work upon the great Boat which lay on Shore upon the Island, but in sight of the Ship; there they hammer'd, and knock'd, and made a Noise, as if they were really caulking and repairing her, in order to her being launch'd off, and put into their Possession. But, towards Night, he oblig'd Gow to write to the Men that Mr Fea would not deliver the Boat till he was in Possession of the Ship; and therefore he order'd them all to come on Shore, without Arms and in a peaceable manner.

This occasioned many Debates in the Ship, but as they had no Officers to guide them, and were all in Confusion, they knew not what to do. So after some time bewailing their hard Fate, and dividing what Money was left in the Ship among them, they yielded, and went on Shore; and were all made Prisoners, to the number of eight and twenty; including those who were secur'd before.

How he brought Gow to be so weak was something strange; Gow being not very supple. But whether it was that he hoped to fare the better for it, and to plead some Merit by obliging his Men to come in without Blood, and perhaps they might encourage him in such Expectations, tho' not promise him, for the last they could not.

Or whether it was that Gow, who knew their Circumstances and Temper also, was satisfy'd if he did not persuade them to it, they would certainly do it without any Persuasion in a Day or two more, having, indeed, no other Remedy, and some of them being really forced Men, desiring nothing more than to surrender.

And if it was neither of these, perhaps Gow, whose Case was now desperate, and who was fully in the Power of his Enemies, and in the Hands of Justice himself, from whom he had indeed no reason to expect any Favour, was, perhaps I say, he was not over desirous to have the rest make their Escape, and therefore was easier to persuade them to put themselves into the same unhappy Circumstances with himself; it being most Natural to People in such Circumstances to desire to have their Comrades ingulpht in the same Misery.

Be it which of these it will, Mr Fea did certainly prevail with Gow to be the Instrument to write to them, and to joyn as it were with Mr Fea's stratagem to draw them on Shore, without which they had not come, at least not at that Time, and so they said afterwards, upbraiding him with having betray'd them; and yet it seems plain too, that when they went they took it for granted that they should be made Prisoners, by their Exclamations one to another, and by their sharing the Money among them, as is said above.

It was indeed a most agreeable sight, to see such a Crew of desperate Fellows so tamely surrender to a few almost naked Countrymen, and to see them so Circumvented by one Gentleman, that were rendered quite Useless to themselves, and to their own Deliverance; the want of a Boat was as much to them as an actual Imprisonment; nay they were indeed in Prison in their Ship, nor was they able to stir one way or other, Hand or Foot; it was too Cold to swim over to the Island and seize the Boat, and if they had, unless they had done it immediately at first, the People on Shore would have been too strong for them; so that they were as secure on board the Ship, as to any Escape they could have made, as they were afterwards in the Condemn'd Hold in Newgate.

Again, never were People more foolishly Circumvented when they had a Boat and Conveniences, for had they gone on Shore then, while they had a Boat, tho' it was but their small Boat, yet going at twice, twenty or five and twenty Men of them, they might have repair'd and launch'd Mr Fea's great Boat, in spite of all he could have done to hinder it, and then, if they could not have got their Ship off, they might have come away, as the Fellows did, with their own Boat, and might soon have found means to get a bigger Boat on the Coast, either of Scotland or England, and getting on Shore in the Night in any convenient Part of England, might have dispers'd and mixt themselves among the People, and made an effectual Escape.

But their End was apparently at hand; Justice was ready for them, their Crimes had ripen'd them for the Gallows, and the Gallows claim'd them; their Time was come, and it was not in their Power to avoid it.

I am longer upon this particular Part because it is so very remarkable, and the Circumstances of it are so unaccountable: That the Boatswain should come on Shore with his Boat, and no more but four Men, thinking to fire and plunder Mr Fea's House with that little Crew; as if he could imagine Mr Fea, who they knew was alarm'd and had been acquainted with what they were, should have no Body at all with him, or that he could storm his House with that little Force.

Then that he should be wheedled into an Ale House by a single Gentleman; as if he would have ventur'd himself into an Ale House with them if he had not had help at Hand to rescue him if any thing had been offered to him.

Then, which was still worse, that they should be taken with the old Bite of having the Gentleman call'd out of the Room, when they were together, as if he could have any Business to talk of there but to lay a Trap for them, and which, if they had their Eyes about them, or, as we might say, any Eyes in their Heads, they might have seen into easily enough.

And to conclude this scene of Madness and Folly together, they came all away and left their Boat, with no Body either in her to keep her a'float, or near her to guard and defend her. Nothing but Men infatuated to their own Destruction, and condemn'd by the visible Hand of Heaven to an immediate Surprise, could have been so stupid; they might have been sure, if there were any People in the Island, they would if possible secure their Boat; and they ought at least to have considered the forlorn Condition of the rest of their Company in the Ship, without a Boat to help themselves: But blinded by their inevitable Fate, in a word, they run into the Snare with their Eyes open; they stood as it were looking on, and saw themselves taken before it was done.

Nay, some of the Men were heard to say, that if their Captain, Gow himself, had but said the Word, they were able to have built a Boat on Board with such stuff as they could have pull'd from the Sides and Ceilings of the Ship, at least big enough to have gone out to Sea, and sailing along the Coast, have either found a better, or seiz'd upon some other Vessel in the Night, or to have made their Escape.

But never Creatures were taken so tamely, trick'd so easily, and so entirely disabled from the least Defence, or the least Contrivance for their Escape; even Gow himself, who, as I said before, never wanted a resolute Courage or Presence of Mind before, and was never daunted by any Difficulties, yet was now snapp'd under a pretence of a Hostage, delivered, and being himself taken and disarm'd, yields himself to be made a Tool of, to bring all the rest to yield at Discretion.

In a word, they were as void of Council as of Courage; they were outwitted on every Occasion; they could not see in the open Day what any one else would have felt in the Dark; but they dropp'd insensibly into Mr Fea's Hand, by one, and two, and three at a time, as if they had told him before hand, that if he went on with his stratagem, he should be sure to have them all in his Custody very quickly; And tho' every one, as fast as they went on shore, were made Prisoners, and secur'd, yet the other were made to believe they were at Liberty, and were simple enough to come on Shore to them.

Every thing we can say of the blindness and folly of these People, who Heaven having determin'd to Punishment, demented and blinded to prepare them for their being brought to it; I say, every thing that can be said to expose their Stupidity and blindness, is a just Panegyrick upon the Conduct of that Gentleman, by whose happy Conduct, and the dextrous Turn he gave to every Incident which happen'd in the whole Affair, was indeed, the principal Means of their being all apprehended.

Had this Gentleman, knowing their Strength and Number was so great, being four times as many Men as he had about him, and better provided for Mischief, than he was for Defence; had he, as it seems others did, fled with his Family over the Firth, or Arm of the Sea, which parted his Island from the rest, by which they had secur'd themselves from Danger; or had he, with the few Men and Fire Arms which he had about him, fortified and defended themselves in his House, and resolv'd to defend themselves there, the Pirates had in all probability gone off again, left him, and made their Escape. Nay, if they had run their Ship a-ground, as they afterwards did, and tho' they had been oblig'd to lay the Bones there, they would, however, have got away some Boat off the Shore, to have made a Long-boat of, and have made their Escape along the Coast, till they came to Newcastle upon Tyne, and there nothing had been more easy than to have seperated and gone to London, some in one Ship, some in another; or, as one of them propos'd, they should have found some Coasting Bark or other riding near the Shore, which they might have boarded, and so gone off to Sea which way they pleas'd.

But they were come a great Way to bring themselves to Justice, and here they met with it in the most remarkable Manner, and with such Circumstances, as I believe are not to be imitated in the World.

When they were all on Shore, and were told that they were Prisoners, they began to reassume a kind of Courage, and to look upon one another, as if to lay hold of some Weapon to resist; and 'tis not doubted but if they had had Arms then in their Hands, they would have made a desperate Defence. But it was too late, the thing was all over, they saw their Captain and all their Officers in the same Condition, and there was no room for Resistance then; all they could have done had been only to cause them to be the more effectually secur'd, and perhaps to have had some or other of them knock'd on the Head for Examples; so seeing there was no Remedy, they all submitted quietly, and were soon dispers'd one from another, till more strength came to carry them off, which was not long.

Thus ended their desperate Undertaking. Heaven having by a visible Infatuation upon themselves, and a Concurrence of other Circumstances, brought them all into the Hands of Justice, and that by the particular Bravery and Conduct of one Gentleman, I mean Mr Fea, who so well manag'd them, that, as above, having at first but five or six Men with him, he brought the whole Company partly by Force, and partly by stratagem, to submit, and that without any loss of Blood on one side or other.

Among the rest of the Papers found on board the Ship, was the following Copy of a Draft, or Agreement of Articles or Orders, or what you please to call them, which were to have been Sign'd, and were for the Direction of the Men, whether on Shore or on Board, when they came to an Anchor in the Orkneys.

They would, I suppose, have been put up upon the Mainmast if they had had longer Time; but they soon found Articles were of no Value with such Fellows; for the going away with the Long-Boat, and ten Men in her, confounded all their Measures, made them jealous and afraid of one another, and made them act afterwards as if they were under a General Infatuation or Possession, allways Irresolute and Unsettled, void of any Forecast or reasonable Actings; but having the Plunder of Mr Fea's House in their View, when they should have chiefly regarded their own Safety, and making their Escape; they push'd at the least significant, tho' most difficult Part, and which was their Ruin in the Undertaking, when they should at first have secur'd their Lives, which, at least to them, was the

Thing of most Value, tho' the easiest at that Time to have secur'd.

By this preposterous Way of Proceeding, they drew themselves into the Labyrinth and were destroy'd, without any possibility of Recovery; nay, they must have perish'd by Hunger and Distress, if there had been no Body to have taken them Prisoners; for having no Boat to supply them with Necessaries, their Ship fast aground upon a barren and uninhabited Island, and no way to be supply'd, they were themselves in the utmost Despair, and I think it was one of the kindest Things that could be done for them, to bring them off, and hang them out of the way.

Their foolish Articles were as follows, viz.:--

I.   That every Man shall obey his Commander in all Respects, as if the Ship was his own, and we under Monthly Pay.

II.   That no Man shall give or dispose of the Ship's Provisions, whereby may be given Reason of Suspicion that every one hath not an equal Share.

III. That no Man shall open or declare to any Person or Persons what we are, or what Design we are upon; the Offender shall be punish'd with Death upon the spot.

IV.   That no Man shall go on Shore till the Ship is off the Ground, and in readiness to put to Sea.

V.   That every Man shall keep his Watch Night and Day, and precisely at the Hour of Eight leave off Gaming and Drinking, every one repair to their respective Stations.

VI.   Whoever Offends shall be punish'd with Death, or otherwise, as we shall find proper for our Interest.

N.B. This Draft of Articles seems to be imperfect, and as it were only begun to be made, for that there were several others intended to be added, but it was suppos'd that their Affairs growing desperate, their Long-Boat gone, and the Boatswain and Boat's Crew, in the Pinnance or smaller Boat gone also, and made Prisoners, there was no more need of Articles, nor would any Body be bound by them if they were made; so the farther making of Orders and Articles were let alone.

These that were made were written with Gow's own Hand, and 'tis suppos'd that the rest would have been done so too, and then he would have taken care to have them executed; but he soon found there was no Occasion of them, and I make no question but all their other Papers and Articles of any kind were destroy'd.

Being now all secur'd and in Custody in the most proper Places in the Island, Mr Fea took care to give Notice to the proper Officers in the Country, and by them to the Government at Edinburgh, in order to get help for the carrying them to England. The Distance being so great, this took up some Time, for the Government at Edinburgh being not immediately concern'd in it, but rather the Court of Admiralty of Great Britain, Expresses were dispatch'd from thence to London, that his Majesty's Pleasure might be known; and in return to which, Orders were dispatch'd into Scotland to have them immediately sent up to England, with as much Expedition as the Case would admit; and accordingly they were brought up by Land to Edinburgh first, and from thence being put on Board the Greyhound Frigate, they were brought by Sea to England.

This necessarily took up a great deal of Time, so that had they been wise enough to improve the Hours that were left, they had almost half a year's time to prepare themselves for Death; tho' they cruelly deny'd the poor Mate a few Moments to Commend his Soul to God's Mercy, even after he was half Murther'd before. I say, they had almost half a year, for they were most of them in Custody the latter end of January, and they were not Executed till the 11th of June.

The Greyhound arriv'd in the River the 26th of March, and the next day came to an Anchor at Woolwich, and the

Pyrates being put into Boats appointed to receive them, with a strong Guard to attend them, were brought on Shore the 30th, convey'd to the Marshalsea Prison in Southwark, where they were deliver'd to the Keeper of the said Prison, and were laid in Irons, and there they had the Mortification to meet their Lieutenant Williams, who was brought home by the Argyle Man of War from Lisbon, and had been committed to the same Prison for a very few days.

Indeed, as it was a Mortification to them, so it was more to him, for tho' he might be secretly pleas'd, that those who had so Cruelly, as he call'd it, put him into the Hands of Justice, by the sending him to Lisbon, were brought into the same Circumstances with himself; yet on the other hand, it could not but be a terrible Mortification to him, that here now were sufficient Witnesses found to prove his Crimes upon him, which were not so easie to be had before.

Being thus laid fast, it remain'd to proceed against them in due form, and this took up some longer time still.

On Friday the 2nd of April, they were all carry'd to Doctors-Commons, where the proper Judges being present, they were Examin'd, by which Examination due Measures were taken for the farther Proceedings; for as they were not equally Guilty, so it was needful to determine who it was proper to bring to an immediate Tryal, and who being less

Guilty, were more proper Objects of the Government Clemency, as being under force and fear, and consequently necessitated to Act as they did; and also who it might be proper to single out as Evidence against the rest; after being thus Examin'd, they were remanded to the Marshalsea.

On the Saturday the 8th of May, the five who were appointed for Evidence against the rest, and whose Names are particularly set down in its Place, were sent from the Marshalsea Prison to Newgate, in order to give their Information.

Being thus brought up to London, and committed to the Marshalsea Prison, and the Government being fully inform'd what black uncommon Offenders they were, it was thought proper to bring them to speedy Justice.

In order to this, some of them, as is said, who were less Criminal than the rest, and who apparently had been forc'd into their Service, were form'd out, and being examin'd, and giving first an Account of themselves, and then of the whole Fraternity, it was thought fit to make use of their Evidence, for the more clear detecting and convincing of the rest. These were George Dobson, John Phinnes, Timothy Murphy, William Booth.

These were the principal Evidence, and were indeed more than sufficient; for they so exactly agreed in their Evidence, and the Prisoners (Pirates) said so little in their

Defence, that there was no room for the Jury to question their Guilt, or to doubt the Truth of any part of the Account given in.

Robert Read was a young Man (mentioned above) who escap'd from the Boat in the Orkneys, and getting a Horse at a Farmer's House, was convey'd to Kirkwall, the chief Town of the said Orkneys, where he surrendered himself. Nevertheless he was brought up with the rest as a Prisoner, nor was he made use of as Evidence, but was try'd upon most, if not all the Indictments, with the rest. But Dobson, one of the Witnesses, did him the Justice to testifie, that he was forced into their Service, as others were, for fear of having their Throats cut, as others had been serv'd before their Faces; and that, in particular, he was not present at, or concern'd in any of the Murthers for which the rest were Indicted; upon which Evidence, he was acquitted by the Jury.

Also be brought one Archibald Sutor, the Man of the House, said above to be a Farm-House, whether the said Read made his Escape in the Orkneys, who testified that he did so Escape to him, and that he begg'd him to procure him a Horse to ride off to Kirkwall, which he did, and that there he surrender'd himself. Also be testified that Read gave him (Sutor) a full Account of the Ship, and of the Pirates that were in her, and what they were; and he (Sutor) discover'd it all to the Collector of the Customs; by which means the Country was allarm'd. And he added, that it was by this Man's means that all the Prisoners were apprehended (tho' that was a little too much too), for 'tis plain, it was by the Vigilance and Courage of Mr Fea chiefly, they were reduc'd to such Distress, as oblig'd them to surrender.

However, it was true that Read's Escape did Allarm the Country, and that he merited very well of the Publick, for the timely Discovery he made. So he came off clear, as indeed it was but Just; for he was not only forc'd to serve them (as above), but as Dobson testified for him, he had often express'd his Uneasiness, as being oblig'd to act with them, and that he wish'd he cou'd get away; and that he was Sincere in those Wishes, as appear'd in that he took the first Opportunity he could get to put it in Practice.

N.B. This Dobson was one of the ten Men who ran away with the Pirates' Long-Boat from the Orkneys, and who were afterwards made Prisoners in the Firth of Leigh, and carryed to Edinburgh.

Gow was now a Prisoner among the rest in the Marshalsea; his Behaviour there was Sullen and Reserv'd, rather than Penitent. It had been hinted to him by Mr Fea, as others, that he should endeavour, by his Behaviour, to make himself an Evidence against others, and to merit his Life by a ready Submission, and obliging others to do the like. But Gow was no Fool; and he easily saw there were too many gone before who had provided for their own Safety at his Expence. And besides that, he knew himself too deeply guilty of Cruelty and Murther, to be expected by the publick Justice as an Evidence, especially when so many others less Criminals were to be had. This, I say, made him, and with good Reason too, give over any Thoughts of Escaping by such means as that. And perhaps seeing so plainly that there was no Room for it, might be the Reason why he seem'd to reject the Offer; otherwise he was not a Person of such nice Honour, as that we should suppose he would not have secur'd his own Life at the Expence of his Comrades.

But, as I say, Gow was no Fool. So he seem'd to give over all Thought of Life, from the first time he came to England; not that he shew'd any Tokens of his Repentance, or any Sence of his Condition, suitable to what was before him. But continuing (as above) Sullen and Reserv'd, even to the very time he was brought to the Bar. When he came there, he could not be try'd with the rest; for the arraignment being made in the usual Form, he refused to Plead. The Court used all the Arguments which Humanity Dictates in such Cases, to prevail on him to come into the ordinary Course of other People in like Government;

laying before him the Sentence of the Law in such Cases; namely, that he must be press'd to Death, the only torturing Execution which remains in our Law; which, however, they were oblig'd to Inflict.

But he continued Inflexible, and carried on his Obstinacy to such a height as to receive the Sentence in Form, as usual in such Cases, the Execution being appointed to be done the next Morning, and he was carried back to Newgate in order to it. But whether he was prevailed with by Argument, and the Reasons of those about him; or whether the Apparatus for the Execution, and the manner of the Death he was to dye, terrified him, we cannot say; but the next Morning he yielded, and petitioned to be allow'd to Plead, and be admitted to be try'd in the ordinary Way; which being granted, he was brought to the Bar by himself, and pleaded, being arraign'd again upon the same Indictment, upon which he had been sentenc'd as a Mute, and was found Guilty.

Williams, the Lieutenant, who, as has been said, was put on Board a Bristol Ship, with orders to deliver him on Board the first English Man of War they should meet with, comes of Course to have the rest of his History made up in this Place.

The Captain of the Bristol Ship, tho' he receiv'd his Orders from the Crew of Pirates and Rogues, whose

Instructions he was not oblig'd to follow; and whose Accusation of Williams, they were not oblig'd to give Credit to; yet punctually obey'd the Order, and put him on Board the Argyle, Captain Bowler, then lying in the Port of Lisbon, and bound for England, who, as they took him in Irons, kept him so, and brought him to England in the same Condition.

But as the Pirates did not send any of their Company, nor indeed could they do it, along with him, to be Evidence against him; and the Men who went out of the Pirate Ship, on Board a Bristol Ship, being till then kept as Prisoners on Board the Pirate Ship, and perhaps could not have said enough, or given particular Evidence sufficient to convict him in a Court of Justice. Providence supply'd the Want, by bringing the whole Crew to the same Place (for Williams was in the Marshalsea Prison before them), and by that means furnishing sufficient Evidence against Williams also, so that they were all try'd together.

In William's Case the Evidence was as particular as in Gow's; and Dobson and the other swore positively, that Williams boasted, that after Maccauly had cut the Super Cargo's Throat imperfectly, he (Williams) did his Business, that is to say, murther'd him; and added, that he would not give him time to say his Prayers, but shot him thro' the Head: Phinnes and Timothy Murphy testifying the same.

And to show the bloody Disposition of this Wretch, William Booth testifyed that Williams propos'd afterwards to the Company, that if they took any more Ships, they should not incumber themselves with the Men, having already so many Prisoners, that in Case of a Fight they should take them and tye them Back to Back, and throw them all over board into the Sea.

It should not be omitted here also in the Case of Gow himself, that as I have observ'd in the Introduction, that Gow had long meditated the kind of Villainy which he now put in Practice, and that it was his Resolution to turn Pyrate the first Opportunity he should get, whatever Voyage he undertook, and that I observ'd he had intended it on Board a Ship in which he came home from Lisbon, but fail'd only for want of making a sufficient Party; so this Resolution of his is Confirm'd by the Testimony and Confession of James Belvin, one of his fellow Criminals, who upon the Tryal declar'd, that he knew that Gow (and he added the Crew of the George Galley) had a Design to turn Pyrates from the beginning, and added, that he discover'd to George Dobson in Amsterdam, before the Ship went out to Sea; for the Confirmation of this, Dobson was called up again, after he had given his Evidence upon the Tryals, and being confronted with Belvin, he did acknowledge that Belvin had said so, and that in particular he had said, the Boatswain and several Others had such a Design, and in especial Manner, that the said Boatswain had a Design to Murther the Master and some others, and run away with the Ship; and being ask'd what was the Reason why he did not immediately Discover it to the Master, Captain Ferneau; he answer'd, that he heard him (Belvin) tell the Mate of it, and that the Mate told the Captain of it; but that the Captain made light of it; but that tho' he was persuaded not to let the Boatswain go along with them, yet the Captain said, he fear'd them not, and would still take him; but that the Boatswain finding himself Discover'd refus'd to go; upon which Gow was named for Boatswain, but was made second Mate, and then Belvin was made Boatswain, and had he been as Honest afterward, as before, whereas on the Contrary, he was as forward and active as any of them, except that he was not in the first Secret, nor in the Murthers, he might have escap'd what afterwards became so justly his Due: But as they Acted together, Justice requir'd they should suffer, and accordingly Gow and Williams, Belvin, Melvin, Winter, Peterson, Rollson, Mackauley, receiv'd the Reward of their Cruelty and Blood at the Gallows, being all Executed together the 11th of June.

N.B. Gow as if Providence had directed that he should be twice Hang'd, his Crimes being of a two-fold Nature, and both Capital; soon he was turn'd off, fell down from the Gibbet, the Rope breaking by the Weight of some that pull'd his Leg to put him out of Pain; he was still alive and sensible, tho' he had Hung four Minutes, and able to go up the Ladder the second Time, which he did with very little Concern'd, and was Hang'd again; and since that a third Time (viz.) in Chains over-against Greenwich, as Williams is over-against Blackwall.

FINIS.

NOTES

by Nigel Rigby

GOW'S CAPTOR:
JAMES FEA OF CLESTRAIN

James Fea's capture of Gow and his crew was a remarkable feat and one for which he deservedly received attention, not all of it welcome. The government awarded him £800 for 'his conduct and good behaviour', as well as £300 for the salvage of the *George Galley* and £400 from the merchants of London, who were well pleased to see the end of Gow's piratical career. In *The Real Captain Cleveland*, James Fea's descendant, Allan Fea, questions whether he ever received the money. He quotes Scott's 'Advertisement' for *The Pirate* which says Fea was:

so far from receiving any reward from the Government that he could not obtain even countenance enough to protect him against a variety of sham suits raised against him by Newgate solicitors, who acted in the name of Gow and others of the pirate crew; and the various expenses, vexatious prosecutions, and other legal consequences in which his gallant exploit involved him, utterly ruined his fortune and his family, making his memory a notable example to all who shall in future take pirates on their own authority.

Fea's financial difficulties were not entirely caused by his capture of Gow, for he also suffered considerably from his espousal of the cause of Charles Stuart, 'Bonnie Prince Charlie', twenty years later. Whether this was due to his resentment at his treatment by the government or to a far deeper conviction is not entirely clear, but the one is not necessarily incompatible with the other and Fea was certainly not alone on Orkney in his Jacobite sympathies. Fea crossed to the mainland to meet Charles Stuart in 1745–6 and offered to supply men and arms in return for an agreement that Charles would address certain grievances if the rebellion were successful. Stuart, not surprisingly, agreed. Equally unsurprisingly, none of Fea's fellow Jacobite sympathisers would openly wed themselves to the Stuart cause and refused to raise troops; Fea was left isolated, his actual contribution to the rebellion amounting in the end to no more than a boat-load of weapons.

In the aftermath of the rebellion, Fea's house on Shap-insay was looted and burnt to the ground by Hanoverian sympathisers, either from malice or because rumours were circulating that the house was being used to hide rebels. Fea himself was not in the house. It took him ten years to get full redress for its destruction.

GOW'S 'ROMANCES'

There is, as I noted in the Introduction, little romance in the story of John Gow, but while missing from *An Account* it is not entirely absent in Orkney traditions which tell of Gow having had affairs with two women: Katherine Rorieson and Helen Gordon. Of the former, John Henderson, author of *Caithness Family History* (1884), writes in his discussion of the Gibson family of Caithness:

> *George, a merchant, who married Katharine, daughter of Bailie Rorison, Thurso. Before her marriage to Mr. Gibson, Katharine Rorison had formed an attachment and engaged herself to John Gow or Smith, a native of*

Scrabster, whose piratical exploits in the early part of last century suggested Sir Walter Scott's tale of "The Pirate". At what period of Gow's career this love affair took place is uncertain, but at any rate the Bailie disapproved of his daughter's choice, and while Gow was absent at sea, obliged her to listen to the addresses of her future husband, then schoolmaster at Stroma. The marriage had scarcely taken place when Gow returned to Thurso, bringing bridal dresses for his betrothed, who, even as matters then stood, would gladly have gone off with him. Gow departed highly incensed, and after Katharine Rorison had settled down in Stroma, he visited the island with the intention of carrying her off, or having his revenge, but he left again without doing any mischief.

The other tradition concerns Helen Gordon, whom Gow may have either known from childhood or met when he returned to Orkney in 1725. In what must have been a whirlwind romance, Gow and Helen are said to have exchanged vows at the Stone of Odin, one of twelve Neolithic standing stones in Stenness, now a World Heritage Site. The Stone of Odin (which was actually demolished shortly after the visit of Sir Walter Scott in 1814 by the tenant farmer who had showed it to Scott, Captain John Sinclair from Caithness) had a hole running right through it and marriage contracts were agreed by the couple clasping hands through the hole. A marriage vow contracted in this way was considered absolutely binding, as much if not more so that an actual marriage: the ceremony, wrote Rev. George Low in 1774, 'was held so very sacred in those times that the person who dared to break the engagement made here was counted infamous, and excluded all society'. It could only be revoked by mutual agreement, the most usual form of which was for the couple to enter the kirk at Stenness, stand back-to-back at the pulpit and leave separately from the north and south doors. After Gow's arrest and dispatch to London for trial, Helen Gordon followed him in order for him to agree to revoke the marriage, only to arrive the day after his execution. Nothing daunted, she went to Execution Dock, waited for low water, touched his dead hand and asked to be released. Sir Walter Scott explained in his 'Advertisement' for *The Pirate*, that 'without going through this ceremony, she could not, according to the superstition of the country, have escaped a visit from the ghost of her departed lover, in the event of her bestowing on any living suitor, the faith which she had plighted to the dead'.

The love affair played a not insignificant part in the story of Gow told to Scott by the aged Bessie Miller, the 'seller of winds', and he incorporated elements of it into

The Pirate through the relationship between the pirate, Captain Cleveland, and Minna Troil. The bleaker narrative of *An Account* describes, briefly, the abduction and rape of three women from Cava (p. 67) who were 'used so Inhumanly, that when [the pirates] set them on Shore again, they were not able to go or stand; and we hear that one of them dyed on the Beach where they left them'. John Russell, the editor of *The Pirate Gow* (1898), notes a variant which appears in the 'First Statistical Account of Orphir' (1834) where 'mention is made of two girls who were taken from the little island of Cava by Gow the pirate. Of them it is said that after spending a few days on board ship, they were returned "to their friends loaded with presents, and they both soon afterwards got husbands."'

RELICS OF JOHN GOW

A number of relics of Gow's return to Orkney still exist in the islands, some in public ownership but most in private hands. A number were listed in the catalogue of Walter Traill Dennison (1825–94), a keen collector of antiquities, relation of Gow's nemesis, James Fea of Clestrain, and a descendant of Jerome Dennison of Warsetter, Sanday, who was present at Gow's capture. I am indebted to Mr Tom Muir of Orkney Museum, Kirkwall for the information on the whereabouts of the relics.

Before the *George Galley*, or *Revenge*, could be floated off the Calf of Eday it had to be lightened and much of the ballast was unloaded and taken ashore. The ballast has been identified by Lynda Bartlett of Orkney Museum as Permian limestone from Sunderland, a globular rock popularly called 'cannonball limestone' from its round inclusions which resemble cannonballs, and it was eventually taken to Kirkwall and incorporated in a tall, pointed spire on a summerhouse being built for the Traill family house (the Traills being one of the leading families on the islands). The house itself burned down in 1938 and was finally demolished during or shortly after the Second World War; the summerhouse then stood in the yard of a factory for many years before being dismantled and rebuilt in 2005 in Tankerness House Gardens behind Orkney Museum in Kirkwall, where it can be seen today.

Carrick House, the Eday home of James Fea, Gow's captor, still has a stain on the floorboards which according to tradition is a bloodstain left by Gow after a failed escape attempt. Indelible stains, like ghosts, are a common enough tradition in ancient houses but some years ago the floorboards were lifted and a black, bitumen-like material found underneath which, when tested, was thought to be blood, so the story may have some truth in it. Carrick House also has a ship's bell bearing the motto *Deo Soli Gloria, 1640* ('glory to God alone') which is said to have been taken from Gow's ship.

Gow's sea chest was appropriated by James Fea's manager, Mr Laing, at the time of his capture and has passed through sale and descent through the Traill and Dennison families until sold to the father of the current owner, Rosemary Jenkins. He loaned it to Stromness Museum shortly after the purchase in 1910, but it was returned to the family in the 1990s. The chest has a spring lock and a shuttle at one end and three compartments containing three large square bottles at the other.

A telescope which is said to have belonged to Gow was also part of Walter Dennison's collection. A photograph of it was reproduced in Allan Fea's *The Real Captain Cleveland* (1912).

SIR WALTER SCOTT'S
THE PIRATE

Scott had only just seen his first novel, *Waverley*, published in the summer of 1814 when he joined the Inspector of Lighthouses for a summer voyage around the coast of Scotland. In August they arrived in Orkney and Scott noted in his diary that:

> we clomb by steep and dirty lanes an eminence rising
> above the town [of Stromness] and commanding a fine
> view. An old hag lives in a wretched cabin on this
> height, and subsists by selling winds. Each captain of a
> merchantman, between jest and earnest, gives to the old

woman sixpence, and she boils her kettle to procure a favourable gale.

The woman, who in selling wind in Orkney was clearly an entrepreneur of some resourcefulness, was called Bessie Miller. Scott thought her 'a miserable figure: upwards of ninety' but she told him a compelling tale about Gow:

who was born near the house of Clestron, and afterwards commenced buccaneer. He came to his native country about 1725 with a snow which he commanded; carried off two women from one of the islands, and committed other enormities. At length, while he was dining in a house in the island of Eda, the islanders headed by Malcolm Laing's grandfather made him prisoner and sent him to London, where he was hanged. While at Stromness he made love to a Miss Gordon, who pledged her faith to him by shaking hands, an engagement which, in her idea, could not be dissolved without her going to London to seek back again her faith and troth by shaking hands with him after execution'.

The details differ from the published *An Account of the Conduct and Proceedings of the Late John Gow*, in which

Helen Gordon does not appear at all, but it is a fair summary of the ill-advised return and arrest of Gow, on which Scott based *The Pirate*. In the 'Advertisement' to the novel, Scott claimed that 'The purpose of the following narrative is to give a detailed and accurate account of certain remarkable incidents which took place in the Orkney Islands'. In fact, Scott's novel bears little resemblance to either the tale he heard from Bessie Miller or the chapter on Gow in *A General History of the Pyrates*, which he read later. Bessie herself, though, plays a key role in the novel as Nona of the Fitful-head, a witch-like figure finally revealed to be the mother of the pirate, Captain Cleveland, who arrives on the islands as the sole survivor from his wrecked pirate ship. Although Cleveland has a 'past' he admits later that in order to survive and prosper as a pirate he had had to suppress his intellect and education in order to command the respect of his crew through bravery, skill and enterprise. Scott's fictional imagination, however, is fired less by piracy than by social and cultural change on Orkney (the theme of old giving way to new is strong in his work) and the novel seems deeply immersed in the tensions between the ancient Norse society and the new order of the incoming Scottish landowners. Scott took some historical liberties here, according to the critics Mark Weinstein and Alison Lumsden, as these social changes had largely been worked through by the time Gow returned to Orkney in 1725.

The Pirate had a mixed reception on publication with some reviewers praising it unreservedly while others felt its descriptive passages to be tedious and the plot complicated and somewhat implausible. Others find the description of the scenery to be 'as graphic and masterly as his best work', while 'the *dramatis personae* will not bear comparison' to his finest fictional characters. More recent critics have noted the difference between Scott's Scottish novels, where his treatment of landscapes and societies was assured, and *The Pirate*, where his unfamiliarity with his subject matter showed through. Confounding his critics, the novel was a success and remained popular throughout the nineteenth century, although it is perhaps less familiar to modern readers.